TEN LITTLE DEMONS

TEN LITTLE DEMONS

Kat, Martin and George receive a mysterious invitation to a social gathering at a beautiful mansion on a secluded island. But when they arrive, they find themselves in the company of an unlikely assemblage of people ... some of whom are not wholly human.

But each has secrets: from the spider-woman to the kitsune; from a mysterious sea captain to a medusa ... ten beings with secrets they would prefer remained hidden ... but when the Fey become involved it's all Kat can do to keep her wits about her.

For the Fey can travel in time, and Kat's adventures are about to become a whole lot stranger ...

A TIME-TWISTING TALE FROM THE AUTHOR OF *ZOMBIES AT TIFFANY'S, KAT ON A HOT TIN AIRSHIP, WHAT'S DEAD PUSSYKAT, KAT OF GREEN TENTACLES* AND *KAT AND THE PENDULUM*

TEN LITTLE DEMONS

TEN LITTLE DEMONS

Sam Stone

Kat Lightfoot Mysteries #6

First published in 2018 by Telos Publishing,
139 Whitstable Road, Canterbury, Kent CT2 8EQ,
United Kingdom

www.telos.co.uk

Telos Publishing values feedback if you have any
comments about this book please email

feedback@telos.co.uk

Huge thanks to:

Paul Cameron, Harvey Clark, Ray Khan,
Steve Matthewman, Katie Meyers, Grace Monroe, Jessica
Shafer, Mervyn Staton, André Tessier and
Alan Roman Walsh for their support of the *Doctor Who*
Merchandise Museum.

This one is for you!

Ten little demons went out to dine;

One choked his little self and then there were nine.

Nine little demons sat up very late;

One overslept himself and then there were eight.

Eight little demons travelling in Devon;

One said he'd stay there and then there were seven.

Seven little demons chopping up sticks;

One chopped himself in half and then there were six.

Six little demons playing with a hive;

A bumblebee stung one and then there were five.

Five little demons going in for law;

One got into Chancery and then there were four.

Four little demons going out to sea;

A red herring swallowed one and then there were three.

Three little demons walking in the zoo;

A big bear hugged one and then there were two.

Two little demons playing with a gun;

One shot the other and then there was one.

One little demon left all alone;

He went out and hanged himself and then there were

none.

Prologue

London, 1865.

'Can I get you anything else tonight, sir?' asked Miss Monroe.

Sir Percival Blackridge looked over the top of his newspaper at his housekeeper. She was a middle-aged woman who had never been married, and Blackridge always wondered why. Miss Monroe was pretty still, she had a petite figure and Blackridge liked the few creases that appeared around her blue eyes when she deigned to smile.

'I'm fine, thank you. I shall retire shortly,' Blackridge said.

Miss Monroe smiled. 'Try not to fall asleep in your study, Sir Percival. Remember the strange dream you had the last time.'

A small flush of red coloured Blackridge's cheeks. He didn't recall telling his housekeeper about his dream. Particularly because she had appeared in it – albeit much younger and far more seductively dressed!

But Miss Monroe was unaware that her comment had raised a brief surge of guilt in her employer, and she went about her business in the same professional manner Blackridge was used to seeing.

When the door to the study closed, Blackridge turned his eyes back to the newspaper and the world's current affairs. It was 20 May 1865 and, following a two-day battle at Palmito Ranch, the American Civil War was finally declared over. News had filtered through from Texas back to New York and finally to London. Blackridge was relieved, because it meant his former trading with the South would soon be able to recommence.

His mind wasn't on the news however. It was on Miss Monroe ... *Grace*. She was often in his thoughts since that night when he had dreamt of her ...

He had woken in his favourite chair in the early hours, disorientated, and taking himself off to bed, had stumbled on the stairs. The next day he had noticed that he had cut his wrist and there were two deep punctures narrowly missing an artery. He had shrugged it off, putting it down to prominent carpet tacks, and after cleaning the wound he had promptly forgotten all about the incident. Until now.

He rubbed the healing scar on his wrist as though it were a new wound that itched.

Blackridge made a point of turning his mind back to the news. He ran a shipping company. Fortunately, he had never dealt in slaves – or, like some of the others who had, the American Civil War would have bankrupted him. Before the war, his merchandise of choice had been fabric, and the South had been his best customers. Of course, it would take some time for them to get back on their feet, but Blackridge was confident that they would. In the meantime, he had provided weaponry to the Northern cause: a venture that had proven very profitable under the circumstances, but he knew would now dry up.

His eyes began to feel tired, but Blackridge pushed on, trying to read the rapidly-blurring words until he couldn't make out anything. He closed his newspaper, folded it and put it down on the small table beside his chair.

The fire was burning down. Blackridge considered putting on another log, but the room was already so warm it was contributing to his drowsiness. He pulled himself upright in his chair, and reached for the glass of brandy on the table beside his newspaper. The glass was empty, but Blackridge couldn't recall finishing it.

'Another nightcap,' he said. Then he stood and made his way over to the bureau by the window. There he poured himself another brandy from the decanter.

The door to the study was open when he turned around.

'I thought Miss Monroe had closed that,' he said to himself.

He walked toward the door, but as he reached it a cold draft brought a shiver to his spine.

Blackridge paused by the door, looking out into the hallway. The house was quiet and very dark. Normally his housekeeper left the gaslights on low so that he could see his way back to his room. Blackridge would usually turn each one off as he passed. But tonight they were all off already.

'Miss Monroe?' he said into the dark.

There was no answer, and Blackridge knew that his housekeeper had long since retired.

It was time for bed anyway.

Blackridge returned to the bureau and put down his brandy glass. He opened the top drawer and took out a candle and matches. Then he lit the candle and turned off the gas light in his office.

The cold breeze continued to waft into his study as

though the London fog had somehow come in from outside. And, with the candlelight, it appeared as though that were the case.

Blackridge considered calling for his footman, as an irrational fear overwhelmed him at the door of his study. He couldn't cross the threshold, and his hallway was now filled with mist.

'Sign it …' a voice said from the dark.

'Who's there?' Blackridge demanded.

The smog wafted deeper into the room. Blackridge backed away, dreading the touch of it. He felt cold. As cold as a corpse, as though his blood was emptying from his veins as he stood there.

'I'm losing my mind,' he said. 'Get a grip, man!'

'Sign …'

Another wave of fog approached him. Blackridge felt his desk against his back, and he turned and hurried around it. Putting the huge mahogany barrier between himself and the smog.

He could see a shape in the vapour. A tall, dark shadow that loomed over his desk wearing a black hooded cowl. A long bony finger pointed to something on the desk. Blackridge saw a stack of papers there that hadn't been present earlier.

'Who are you?' he asked.

'Sign …' said the voice again.

Blackridge knew who stood over him then. It was death, and its breath was as foul as the London mist it brought in with it.

Blackridge found a pre-inked quill in his hand, and his fingers moved of their own volition, swirling around on the paper on a dotted line he couldn't see but knew was there.

'What am I signing?' he said.

'Your last will and testament,' said the voice.

Blackridge dropped the quill, but the deed was done, and the creature whipped away the papers before he could react. He was left shuddering as the smog retreated, taking the hooded figure with it.

Blackridge woke. He was sleeping by the dying embers of the fire, and he felt chilled to the bone. He looked around his study. The gas was still lit and the door was firmly closed. Feeling disorientated, he stood up and looked around the room. Everything was normal. As it had been before he fell asleep. Now Miss Monroe's warning echoed in his mind. She was right. He did have unusual dreams whenever he nodded off there.

Time for bed. He shuddered again as though these words echoed into his mind with the remnants of his dream.

Blackridge stood up and walked to the study door. He looked out on the hallway, lit as it was by the gaslight – turned down low, as it always was.

He shook away the awful dream. It had been a nightmare for certain, but relevant nonetheless, as he had recently asked his lawyers to draw up his will. It was as yet unsigned, and Blackridge's dream was a way of reminding him that, like all men of middle age, he must get his affairs in order. His nephew was the sole beneficiary of course. Blackridge had never married, and had no children.

He glanced over at his desk and saw the will sitting there. He would read it and attend to it first thing.

He turned to the gaslight, and as he switched it off, his eyes fell on the bureau and the decanter: his brandy glass stood beside it, half-filled. Blackridge knew the glass had been on the table by his newspaper before he had fallen asleep.

Now he questioned himself. Had he stood and poured another drink?

He looked back at the will on his desk. Maybe he should take care of this now?

'Sir Percival?' a voice said behind him.

He turned to find Miss Monroe by the door.

'Is everything all right?' she asked.

'Yes. I nodded off. Had a silly dream again!' he laughed.

'It's always that way,' she said. 'Now maybe you should retire for the night?'

Blackridge nodded and hurried past her. As he reached the first light, he reached up to turn it off.

'Sir Percival? Your drink …'

Miss Monroe passed Blackridge his brandy glass.

'Ah yes … Shame to waste it,' he said.

'I was sorry to hear of the death of your uncle,' said Daniel Tovey of Tovey, Reign and Handcock Solicitors.

'I understand you handled his last will and testament,' Richard Blackridge said. 'My uncle told me to contact you in the event of his death. I know it was several weeks ago, but I was in New York on business and I've only just returned.'

'Ah, yes,' said Tovey. 'I'm afraid I can't help you.'

'What do you mean?'

'Your uncle did ask us to prepare a will, and then it seems he changed his mind. This one was brought to us following his death. His estate has now been handed over to the beneficiary.'

Tovey placed a neat pile of papers on top of his desk.

'But … *I* am the beneficiary,' Richard said.

'I'm afraid he left everything to his new wife …'

'*Wife*? But there must be a mistake: my uncle never married.'

Tovey showed Richard the marriage certificate and the will.

'But … he told me before the trip that everything would be left to me. I am running the business in America for him,' said Richard. 'Who is this woman? Where did she come from? What would she know about his professional affairs?'

'It must have been one of those whirlwind things,' said Tovey. 'But the will states she must have full control of everything. And I'm afraid that Lady Blackridge has informed me that your services are longer required.'

'No longer required! Why, I must speak with her at once!'

'I'm sorry, but I have no idea how to contact her. She fired me too.'

'Then I'll go to the house …'

'I did the very same thing a week ago. The house is closed and up for sale.'

'This woman marries my uncle, he dies, and she inherits everything. Then she just sells up and leaves. How is this possible in so short a time? Why is Scotland Yard not investigating this? Don't you think it suspicious?'

'Most unfortunate,' Tovey said. 'But I'm sorry. There is nothing I can do.'

Despite the lawyer's words, Richard Blackridge travelled to the former house of his uncle. He stood on the pavement, looking up at the shuttered windows. There was a sign marking the house sold. Even so, Richard rang the doorbell. Then banged on the front door. No-one answered, but he was desperate.

'Miss Monroe! It's Richard Blackridge here. Please may I speak to you?'

He hammered on the door harder.

'No use. She's long gone, sir,' said a voice behind him.

Richard stopped knocking and turned to see the butler of the house next door.

'Do you know where she is?' he asked.

The butler shook his head.

'I have to find her!'

'I'm sorry, sir …'

Blackridge walked away from the house. He had a little money left, but what he had would barely put a roof over his head for a few days.

'How did this happen?' he wondered.

1

New York, 1867

'Is this the boat to Canarsie Pol?' I asked.

'Yes, miss. I'm Captain Carey. Welcome aboard.' Carey held out his hand and helped me board.

'Can I take your bag, miss?'

'No, thank you,' I said. 'I'll keep this. But my carriage-driver will bring on my trunk.'

I placed my carpet bag down on the deck by my feet. Inside were a few changes of clothes and my weapons and gadgets. I looked around the boat and found it empty bar one person.

'Martin! What are you doing here?'

'Pepper sent for me,' Martin said. 'I assume he also sent for you?'

'Yes,' I nodded, and turned my face away to hide the slight flush that coloured my cheeks.

I had received a note from our mutual colleague George Pepper asking me to join him on a private island for a party he had been invited to. I must admit the invitation had thrown me a little. Until I saw Martin I had foolishly believed that this was not a demon-slaying call to arms but a call into Pepper's arms … I weighed up my emotions. I was torn between disappointment and relief.

Pepper and I had been dancing around each other since our last adventure in Spain. We had pretended to be man and wife while investigating the death of Martin's sister and had learnt a lot about each other during that time. As a result, our relationship was forever altered, but neither of us was ready to make the first move to take things to the next stage. Going from comrades-in-arms to lovers meant a lot of changes. What if things didn't work out? We had been in that awkward situation before, and I didn't want to hurt Pepper like that again. I had to be sure, and so did he, that we were really willing to take our relationship into different territory.

Martin knew this, and conscientiously ignored it as any real friend might do. He knew better than to involve himself in our personal struggles: Pepper and I were attracted to each other, there was no point in denying it anymore, but we were still trying to face up to the implications of this attraction. It wouldn't be an easy road forward, but we were good at distracting ourselves from traversing it. After all, there was always a demon to slay, a city to save, and a hell dimension to prevent from escaping into our world.

You see, my name is Kat Lightfoot, and I'm a demon slayer. I work with an inventor called Martin Crewe and an ex-soldier, George Pepper. Both are my friends. Though Pepper could be so much more.

'So, what did Pepper's note say?' Martin said.

'Just to meet him at the island. A party or something,' I said.

'Hmmm. He must be onto something,' Martin said.

A few more people joined us on the boat. Martin and I kept to ourselves, and oddly so did the new arrivals.

None of them seemed to know each other. We were the exceptions.

The island was in Jamaica Bay and was known as Canarsie Pol. We had always believed it was uninhabited, and it was a surprise to learn that this was not the case at all.

'So, who owns this place?' I asked Captain Carey.

'Mr Black,' he said. 'He built the house several years ago. He's some English businessman, and this is his holiday get-away.'

'And you work for him?' Martin said.

'Sometimes …'

'What's he like?' I asked.

'Who?' said Carey.

'Mr Black,' Martin said.

'Dunno. Never seen him.'

I was a little surprised by Carey's words. It was odd that the owner had never travelled to his own home via this boat.

'But … you must have brought him in,' said Martin.

'As far as I know, he's never been here. Though I believe he will be this weekend. I'm booked to collect him and bring him across later today. But usually I just bring provisions for the caretaker and his wife.'

This was an unusual weekend indeed if the house was being opened to guests for the very first time and its owner was also making his first visit. This led once more to the question – who were these people? And, more importantly, why were we there?

There were three women and seven men on board with us. All of them had found their own quiet space on the boat. Some watched as we crossed the water and approached the island. Others sat in quiet contemplation. I decided I'd take the bull by the horns and just introduce myself. But as this thought occurred to me, I realised that the boat was already pulling in at a small, rickety pier.

Carey jumped off onto the jetty and tied up. Then he positioned a small gangplank across the breach. He held out his hand and helped one of the three women to cross.

'Miss Monroe,' he said, bowing his head a little. 'Mr Black said there are instructions for you in the house.'

'Thank you,' she said, and without waiting for her luggage she scurried off.

It appeared that Carey knew everyone's names. As they crossed the gangplank, either with or without his assistance, he nodded politely and addressed them all.

'Mr Clark, Mr Cameron, Miss Meyers, Mr Khan, Mr Matthewman, Mr Walsh, Miss Shafer, Mr Staton,' and finally, 'Mr Tessier.'

I waited back with Martin. We hadn't been invited by the owner, so we weren't expecting the captain to know us.

'Good day, Miss Lightfoot ... Mr Crewe,' he said politely. 'Have a pleasant stay.'

I didn't ask how the captain knew our names but assumed that we were indeed on the invitation list after all. Then I turned to look up the pathway that all of the other guests had taken, and I saw the shape of the house looming on the horizon. With the sun directly behind it, it was difficult to make out the features beyond the shape, but I could tell that the property was unusual for a home off the shores of Brooklyn. I would have expected something colonial in style, but instead it was made of brick and resembled houses that might be found in Europe. It was castle-like, with turrets and what appeared to be a roof-top walkway. The house was huge, and obviously had enough space to accommodate the hosts, their staff and the guests that had been invited. My curiosity was piqued further.

As we walked upwards I thought I saw two figures bobbing down between the rocks above the house.

Martin and I walked up the pathway and found a set of steps that led along the rock-face up to the front door. The door was painted blood red. There was a ring-pull bell, but the door stood open and a middle-aged butler waited beside it with a woman in a cook's uniform.

'Miss Lightfoot, Mr Crewe,' said the man. 'I'm Edward Brewster, your butler, and this is Cerys Brewster, my wife and the housekeeper and cook.'

'Hello,' I said. 'You were expecting us?'

'Of course. Mr Black said that Mr Pepper's friends would be here also. May I take your bag?'

'No,' I said.

Brewster laughed. 'Mr Black said you would say that.'

'Who is Mr Black?' Martin asked.

'Why, he is the owner of the house, and your host for the weekend. Please do come in. Mrs Brewster will show you to your rooms.'

We had entered a large hallway decorated in a very European traditional style. The walls were plastered and a picture rail ran around the edge of the room. The colour scheme was duck egg blue below the rail and white above. There was ornate coving all around the ceiling corners and around the large crystal chandelier that dropped down into the centre of the hallway between two staircases. The stairs circled from either side to meet on a half landing in the middle, then separated once more and went to opposite landings. North and south wings. This was indeed a very big house. But I was pleased to see it more modern and less gothic castle inside, despite its exterior appearance.

'This way,' said Mrs Brewster, and Martin and I

followed her up the stairs and to the left. We, it seemed, were to be in the north wing.

'Here you are, miss,' said Mrs Brewster. She pushed open a door, curtseyed and then led Martin away to the room next door.

'Mr Pepper is across the way,' she said over her shoulder.

I went into the room and looked around. It was bright and sunny with the curtains open, and that same egg shell blue covered the walls. There was a mahogany wardrobe on one side, along with a dresser with mirror and stool and a small chest of drawers, on which stood a pitcher of water and a wash bowl.

My trunk was already at the bottom of the bed, and I wondered how that could be, so quickly, and how the captain had managed to pass us without us seeing him.

A knock at the door announced a visitor, and I opened it to see Pepper looking fresh-faced and happy.

'Wait until you see this place,' he said. 'There's a nice little island to explore too.'

He took my hand and pulled me from the room, still carrying my carpet bag – which is rarely ever out of my sight, because it contains my demon-slaying weaponry.

'Why do we always end up in big castles or mansions? And what's the score here?' I asked.

'It's a party,' said Pepper. 'And we've been invited.'

We went downstairs and found the other invitees gathering in the huge hallway. Brewster walked around with a tray and offered canapés while Mrs Brewster served champagne in tall flutes.

'Mr Black welcomes you! I'm Grace Monroe, Mr Black's assistant.'

The hairs stood up on the back of my neck as I looked at Grace. She was tall, willowy, slender and very attractive, and she was wearing a formal travelling suit made of velvet.

'A little light refreshment,' she said. 'While we all introduce ourselves. Then we'll dress for dinner. Mr Black should be here by then too.'

The hallway was bright and sun shone into the room from two large windows, but Grace Monroe had her own illumination. I glanced at Pepper and saw him watching her with an awestruck expression. Then, as I looked around the room, I noticed that everyone there was admiring her in the same way. Was it only I who was not so taken with Grace? There was something off about her. Though I wasn't sure what. Yet.

I took Pepper's hand, and he glanced at me in a daze, and then I saw his eyes clear. Whatever mystical hold Grace had, it had started to diminish with my touch. Interesting.

I turned and looked at one of the tall windows that flanked the front door. Something had caught my eye. I stared at the window for a long time, but nothing moved. It had probably been a seagull flying past, but I felt a little niggle of insecurity at the thought of being watched by an unseen person.

'I don't see the fascination,' a voice said beside me. I looked at the man. He was tall, slender, elegant. He held the champagne glass with the style and class that showed good breeding. He was also English.

'Paul Cameron,' he said.

Pepper shook Paul's hand. Then Paul took mine and placed a gentlemanly kiss on my gloved fingertips.

'Miss Lightfoot, I presume?' Paul said.

'How do you know?' I asked.

'Dear lady, I made it my business to find out everything I could about all of the people on Black's invitation list.'

'Do you know Mr Black?' Pepper asked.

'Not personally. But we've done business together via third parties. I must admit I was surprised to receive the invitation. Black is an infernal snob, and I don't come under the bracket of high society associates, merely business ones.'

'What is it you do, Mr Cameron?' I asked.

'I deal in … medicine,' he said.

Before I could question him further, Grace approached us again, with another man at her side. 'Miss Lightfoot, may I introduce you to Mr Clark?' she said. 'He's English too.'

'And you're from New York,' Pepper said, 'if I read the accent correctly? But there's a trace of something else …'

'I lived in England for a time,' Grace said. 'It's where I was when Mr Black engaged me as his assistant.'

'Tell us about Mr Black,' said Martin, appearing beside us.

'He's a very wealthy gentleman, who's turned his hand to business,' Grace said.

'He's English too?' asked another man, joining our group.

'Everyone, this is Mr Steven Matthewman. He's English as well … Quite a few of the guests are. But in answer to your question: Mr Black has never told me his origins. Though he could be English.'

Pepper shook Matthewman's hand, and then Matthewman went through the process of kissing the hands of the women. But when his lips touched my fingers the hairs stood up on my arms and at the back of my neck. I noticed then that Matthewman had a glow that was different from Grace's; there was something very animalistic about him. I didn't know what it was. But the intoxicating scent of wild forests came from the man.

My cat senses tingled around him, and I saw him frowning as he quickly dropped my hand. It was obvious that he'd had some sort of reaction to our contact too.

'What is it you do, Mr Clark?' he asked, turning now to the quiet gentleman who had been introduced just before he himself had stepped forward.

'Mr Clark is a Captain of a sea vessel called *The Siren*,' Grace cut in. 'Mr Black tells me you're very reserved, Mr Clark, so I hope you don't mind my speaking for you.'

Clark nodded his head, giving Grace his approval, and took a sip of his champagne. He didn't speak, so I could only speculate as to where he was from.

'Over here is Miss Jessica Shafer …' Grace said.

We turned our heads in unison to see Jessica. She was dressed sombrely, as though she had just attended a funeral.

'Miss Shafer was a nanny. But I believe she retired when she recently became a woman of means …'

Jessica looked at us coldly. Her stare could turn a man or woman to stone.

'My private affairs are not for discussion, Miss Monroe,' she said. 'Now, if you'll all excuse me, I'll go and change for dinner.'

I watched Jessica go back upstairs with a great deal of curiosity. Though perfectly normal in looks, she was a strange woman who moved with a rolling gait that was somewhat reptilian.

'Perhaps we should all retire for a short time when we've finished our introductions,' Grace said.

'I'm Ray Khan,' said a man wearing very unique garb: he was dressed in a gold-coloured smoking jacket over red satin pantaloons. His appearance was a mixture of styles, oriental, British, Indian perhaps. All of it suggested an occupation with travel.

'Mr Black tells me you're an inventor,' said Grace.

'Of sorts,' Khan said.

'And who is this gentleman?' I asked.

'Mervin Staton at your service, Miss Lightfoot,' said the man. He bowed low over my hand. 'And may I present Miss Katie Meyers?'

'Mr Staton deals with retirement investments,' Grace said. 'And Miss Meyers is a Girl Scout Leader. No doubt you've heard of the movement?'

'We call them Girl Guides in Britain,' said the final guest. Grace introduced him as Alan Roman Walsh. A retired police detective from Scotland Yard.

'But what brings you into Mr Black's company?' asked Pepper.

'What brought any of us here?' replied Walsh.

2

After dressing for dinner in a purple velvet gown, I stowed several weapons from my carpet bag about my person. A laser gun in one boot, a diamond shard dagger in the other. In a hidden pocket in my gown I had access to my full weapons belt, which was hidden under the bulk of the skirt. The skirt itself could be removed with a quick tug at the waist to release the pin holding it in place, and underneath I wore my usual men's breeches for comfort and emergencies.

Ready, I left my room, crossed the hallway and tapped on Pepper's door.

'Do you want to give me a clue what's going on?' I asked.

'Let's go to Martin's room to talk,' he said.

It wasn't like Pepper to be so nervous around me, but after our last adventure I suppose we were still a little awkward with each other. A situation that might continue if we didn't finally talk about it. But that wasn't our way. We liked to try to ignore our feelings.

Martin opened the door just as we arrived.

'Come in,' he said.

Pepper and I entered and Martin closed the door.

Martin's room was similar to mine except that it had a fireplace. Next to it was a bell-pull that I assumed summoned the serving staff.

'So,' I said, getting straight to the point, because I hate to waste time, 'what do we know about this Mr Black?'

'Not much,' said Pepper. 'He's a wealthy gentlemen, who's turned his hand to business …'

'Hmm. Just the official line that Miss Monroe gave, then? Do we know, what type of business?' I asked.

'Judging by the people he's invited, his interests are quite diverse. There's a man who deals in medicine, a police officer, a judge, a former nanny and a Girl Scout leader. As well as a ship's captain, a mysterious gentleman who hails, if I'm not mistaken, from India … and no-one mentioned what Mr Matthewman does, so he is a complete mystery. None of these people, I'm sure, has actually ever met Black in person.'

'Why do you think that?' asked Martin.

'Even Miss Monroe hasn't met him,' Pepper said. 'He's engaged her, but from a distance.'

'She told you that?' I asked.

'In a fashion. Remember how she avoided the question of what Black looked like by switching our attention to each other.'

'Mmmm … The introductions did seem a little …' I said.

'Strange?' said Pepper.

'Yes,' Martin and I said in unison.

'And with a little too much information added in places,' I said.

'She didn't introduce any of us in the same way, though. But everyone knew who we were,' Pepper said.

'I noticed that too,' said Martin. 'Which does beg the question, *how*?'

We debated this for a few minutes without conclusion. We demon-slayers kept our business private, and it wasn't likely that any time soon we'd be discussing our affairs with total strangers. But what if this house full of strangers already knew what we did for a living?

'Anyone find anything strange about Grace?' I said. 'And Matthewman also?'

'Grace is very attractive. Hypnotically so,' said Martin. 'I was taken in by it for a time, but then shook off the effects. It was as though the air was filled with some kind of scent at the time, too.'

'I smelt it as well,' said Pepper. 'Very *exotic* … Then Kat took my hand and I came to my senses.'

'Some creatures are known to give off a scent to attract a mate,' Martin said.

'There was definitely attraction involved,' Pepper said. Then he gave a little cough as though he were embarrassed by his initial reaction to Grace.

'She was attractive to everyone but me and Mr Cameron,' I said. 'What about Matthewman? My cat senses kept telling me to flee.'

'Interesting,' said Pepper. 'Did you have any other reaction?'

'He smelt of nature. Forests. Trees. That kind of thing,' I said.

Martin nodded, 'I got a waft of that too from him. What do you think it means?'

'There's a supernatural element in play here. Otherwise we wouldn't have been invited along.'

'Have we been commissioned to investigate?' Martin asked.

'No. We received the invitation just like everyone else.'

'We can only wonder then at the agenda,' I said.

The bell-pull moved by the fireplace and a ringing

sound echoed through Martin's room.

'I didn't know those things worked both ways ...' I said.

'They don't usually. Though, I think that is our warning that dinner is ready,' said Martin.

We walked down the staircase together and met up with the other guests once more in the hallway. This time there was another man, standing by the dining room door.

He was very tall. Wearing a dinner suit and a cloak, as though he had just been outside on a cold night and couldn't get warm.

'Who's that, I wonder?' I said.

'The Great Inspiro,' said Merv Staton behind me. 'Otherwise known as André Tessier. He's a magician who is purported to have genuine magical ability.'

Tessier glanced over at us as though he'd heard Staton's whispered explanation.

'Dinner is served, everyone!' said Grace.

After dinner the men took brandy and cigars in the dining-room and I was left with Grace, Katie and Jessica in the parlour. Brewster came round with a tray of glasses and a decanter of port.

'As you requested ...' he said, placing it down beside me. Then he left the room again. He looked flustered, and I think it was because he and his wife were unused to having quite so many guests at once.

'I'm not much of a smoker,' said Cameron, coming into the room with a glass of brandy in his hand. 'And male company has a tendency to bore me, especially when the ladies have far more to say.'

I smiled at him and he came and sat beside me.

'Have we met before?' I asked him.

He reminded me of an urban fox I'd seen once. Cameron did not appear to be a Kitsune, though; he was British, not Japanese, and I had never known them to be of any other nationality.

Cameron eyes were yellow in the candlelight, though, and they reflected something dark into the room. A little like the Kitsune had. Was this some demon offspring whose origin I had yet to learn?

'You are curious about me, Miss Lightfoot?' he said, as though he could read my mind.

'Is it so obvious?' I said.

'Not as obvious as why Mr Black invited you and your colleagues here,' Cameron said.

'It isn't obvious to me,' I said.

'Look again,' he said.

I glanced over at Grace and Jessica playing cards and Katie standing by the door apart from them. She watched the other two women with a wary expression.

I peered at Grace first, seeing something in her that I hadn't before. Did she have multiple eyes?

Jessica slapped down a card on the table and I glanced at her again. She smiled, her tongue flicked out. It was forked.

'Grace is a Black Widow,' said Cameron. 'Jessica, a Medusa. Though she's keeping her snakes in tonight or we'd all be turned to stone.'

I sat back in my chair. Now that Cameron had pointed it out, it was obvious. I'd come across a Medusa a couple of years before, when Martin had experimented with time travel and we had ended up in the 21st Century for a few months.[1] Such a creature was draining the life from its victims, turning them initially to stone. Then the dead mysteriously revived and began to pass this virus on to others. The Medusa strain was dangerous. Only an original, as Jessica obviously was, could sustain their life-force without regular feeding. Only an original could hide and control the head full of snakes whose glare could turn a person to stone. But those infected by an original or another carrying the virus had to kill, or they turned back to stone, then crumbled to dust.

I turned my attention to Grace. The Black Widow was unusual. I'd never seen one of her type before. I asked Cameron what she was.

'She's a spider with a difference,' he said. 'She spins a web of illusion around her victims until she gets all she needs from them.'

'What is it she needs?'

'In her case … their wealth; and usually that means an end to their life too.'

'And you?' I asked.

'You've already guessed what I am. *Kitsune*. We did almost meet once. In a very dark alley behind the medicine shop of one of my cousins.'

'I thought so,' I said. 'I rarely forget a face, even in shifted form.'

'Neither do I, and you are somewhat *infamous*, Miss Lightfoot.'

I didn't ask him to explain his comment as I recalled our previous meeting. I had been stalking the backstreets of New York. For a time I'd been captured by the fox's

---

[1] See *Four Weddings and a Demon Slayer*. Available in *The Complete Kat Lightfoot* deluxe hardback.

beautiful eyes as they had reflected the gaslight from the nearby street. Then I'd heard a howl from a few blocks away – it had come from the creature I'd been tracking. I had looked away from the fox in the direction of my prey, then back. The fox had gone, but a man had stood in the shadow of the back door of a shop. The door had opened. The man had gone inside. I hadn't seen him properly, but I knew he had been a Kitsune: a shape-shifter of Japanese origin.

'But you, sir, are not Japanese!' I pointed out.

Cameron dropped the Englishman façade, and sitting next to me was an old Japanese man with a fox-like face. Then he restored the glamour, returning almost immediately to the appearance of the British gentleman.

'I'm less conspicuous this way,' he said.

Pepper, Martin and the other men returned to the drawing-room smelling of cigar smoke. One glance at Pepper told me he had learnt a significant amount while spending time with the other men.

Tessier was the last of them to enter, and he sat apart from the others, by the fire, and gazed into the flames without speaking to anyone.

Then Brewster came into the room wheeling a trolley that held a gramophone. We fell silent as he placed a record on the turntable and then cranked the handle several times. The table began to spin, and Brewster moved the needle to the start of the recording.

'Splendid!' said Grace. 'I hope you have something entertaining on that, Brewster!'

Germanic music blasted out of the machine and then faded.

'Welcome all to my home,' said a gravelly voice.

'That's … Mr Black!' said Grace.

'By now you will be beginning to realise that this is no

ordinary place, and that you are with a group of extraordinary beings. Let me introduce you properly to your fellow guests. First, my assistant, the Black Widow, Miss Monroe. What a beguiling creature; but don't fall foul of her charms, lest you become her next victim. How many men have you preyed on, Grace? Twenty? Thirty?'

'That's not true!' gasped Grace. Then she laughed. 'Why … this is a joke, surely?'

'Of course she will deny it,' continued Black. 'But let me reveal, her latest victim died just three short weeks before I engaged her to work for me. By then, she had liquidated the man's assets, taking the livelihood from his nephew, who was made destitute by her gain. I've kept her out of trouble these last three years because she was hoping to line me up as her next conquest. Fortunately, I am immune to her charms.'

Grace had fallen quiet. Now everyone's eyes turned to her.

'Then there is Mr Tessier. The Great Inspiro! A magician, but really a man who practices the dark arts. He is not to be trusted. This man opened a portal to a cosmic dimension allowing monstrosities through that disguised themselves as gods and prayed on humanity. Many people have died because of him.'

Tessier stood up and glared at the gramophone. 'Shut that thing off!' he said.

'It is my wish that this machine not be touched,' Black said, as though he had known that Tessier would respond this way. *'Brewster has my permission to stop anyone who tries.'*

I looked at Brewster. The man was now holding a weapon in each hand. Two thick black pistols of unknown origin and unknown firepower.

'What of Mr Staton?' Black continued. *'A former judge. Corrupted. Paid by the rich to condemn the poor. Many a young man was sent to the colonies because of him. But I speak*

of one man now. Found guilty of a crime he didn't commit. Staton had him hanged. The man's wife and child starved to death, unable to survive. A vile crime, with such terrible effects. All of his sentences had consequences for which he must now pay.'

'Ridiculous!' said Staton. 'Convicting criminals is my duty.'

'Miss Meyers. What an unusual creature you are. You work with children. Little girls whom you care for with such profound attention. But what of the many tiny babes you've stolen away to the underground? The Unseelie Court has you to thank for more than half of its cherubs. Oh, the parents didn't miss these babes. Changelings were left in their place. They grew as children do, but they were all empty shells, phantoms shaped in the image of a person, destined to live a cold and empty life. Their parents, never knowing the exchange that had been made, despaired at the strangeness of their unemotional children. But I do not expect remorse from you, Miss Meyers. That is not the way of the Sidhe.'

'I do not deny that I am Fae,' said Katie. 'I am proud that I come from an old and ancient family.'

'Then of course there is you, Mr Matthewman. A man by day, a wolf on the full moon. Responsible for the death of an entire family and all of their farmhands. You feasted well the night you turned.'

'वेयरवोल्फ!2' said Khan.

'I don't deny what I am either. Only to say this curse was put on me. If I could shirk it I would. For I have no joy in taking lives!'

'The wolf in you does, though,' Cameron said.

'Mr Clark is next. A dark and insidious character. If he opens his mouth to speak, then I recommend you cover your

---

2 Hindi. Pronounced: veyaravolph. Meaning: werewolf.

ears. *Mr Clark is Mer. King of them all, in fact. He is driven onto land every seven years when his fins turn to limbs. His skin becomes pale and human. He is incapable of speech, able only to sing his siren song. Until such a time that his seduction of hapless females gives him the power to return. There he replenishes his harem with this new breeding stock. For, on hearing his song, no woman can resist the call. Once under the water they are condemned to remain until they die.'*

Clark, fortunately, didn't sing. Perhaps we women present were not 'good' breeding stock.

'Mr Khan of course has a secret too. He has his own vessel, many fathoms down. His real name is Nemo, and he was a prince on land until he cast off the world for the sea. What crimes he's done to man and sea creature since then can only be described as immoral.'

'The Saabs who took hold of my country are the criminals, not I. Anyone I destroyed on my flight deserved it for their crimes against my people.'

'*Nemo,*' Black's voice echoed from the gramophone.

The needle reached the end of the record. Then Brewster stepped forward and changed it, cranking the handle several times again.

'Then we come to Miss Shafer, who is of course a vicious killer. Known to turn her victims to stone for the sheer pleasure of seeing them die. Shafer is as cold as marble, containing a heart that is frozen. Like the others here, she has no remorse for her crimes. Even for causing a Medusa epidemic on a small island in the Caribbean. An island now full of statues – once human. They crumble to dust at the slightest touch.'

Jessica shrugged, showing her indifference to Black's accusation.

'I turn now to Mr Cameron. A Kitsune. A medical man. Meant only to bring about good to this world. But not this man. He leads his patients down a dark path, following the dragon into another realm. An innocent girl recently suffered at his

hands. So addicted was she to his opium infusions, that she never wanted to leave that realm. She wasted away and was found in a pile of her own faeces, starved of nutrition. She failed to come round even to drink. No-one attended her as she remained locked in a dark cell under Cameron's shop. The opiate was fed in through a vent, sucking away her very soul into that dark world that only the Kitsunes know of.'

'It's against my creed,' Cameron denied. 'To do such a thing. I suspect Black has me confused with another creature.'

'Amongst this demon horde are humans too. Alan Roman Walsh. Former Detective of Scotland Yard. Walsh made his fortune being bribed, and then the mistake of taking out a loan. His failing was when he approached a Night Shade. And, for those of you who know little of this creature, it lives within the realms of shadow, only free to roam at night. Walsh failed to pay back the hefty toll levied by the Shade. Now he pays the price. Once a month, in the shadow of night, Walsh is forced to transform into a Shade. His only way to return to human form is to suckle on the soul of an innocent. If he fails to do this by sun up, he remains a Shade forever. Living neither in this realm, nor in the other. An exile from both.

'So, Walsh chooses to take the breath of the newborn to preserve his own pitiful life.'

Walsh sipped his brandy. 'I didn't ask to be cursed,' he said. 'Anyone of you would do the same.'

'I don't think we would,' said Pepper.

'And then I come to our trio of Demon Slayers. Miss Lightfoot – only partly human herself. She is a cat-vampire hybrid.'

The demons in the room shrank back from me as though my touch could severely damage them. And probably my bite could. I smiled, flashing fangs, for the fun of it. It wouldn't hurt for them to know I was dangerous as well.

'In truth, Lightfoot does not know what she is. But she and her colleagues are responsible for the deaths of many demons. Some of whom wanted only to hide out in the human realm. They did no harm beyond what their nature dictated.'

'That's a matter of opinion,' said Pepper.

'And Pepper. Adorer of Lightfoot, he'll risk life and limb and even his soul to follow wherever she leads.'

I looked at Martin, trying to gage his reaction to Black's words.

'Martin Crewe is the gooseberry in their apple pie. But he has his uses. And his gadgets have expelled the souls of many a demon back to hell.'

'You say that like it's a bad thing, Black,' Martin said, as though expecting the record to answer.

'And so my introductions conclude ...' Black said. *'Enjoy each others' company. It won't last long. In case you haven't realised, you've all been brought here to die ...'*

I found myself staring at the gramophone as it continued to turn. Silence, followed by the *tic tic tic* of the needle against the end of the groove. 'I take it Mr Black won't be joining us then, after all,' I said.

The Great Inspiro took a sip of his brandy, swallowed wrong and then began to cough.

Cameron patted the man on the back. Inspiro's cough turned into a frantic gasping and choking. Then the magician slumped back in his chair, and there was an immediate transformation in him. His wide-open eyes appeared to water and then turn glassy, bulging a little from their sockets. Then his lips parted and his tongue, swollen and blue, protruded from them.

'He's dead!' said Cameron.

Martin took the man's pulse. 'I'd advise that no-one drinks or eats anything unless they prepare it themselves.'

'Poison?' I asked.

'More than likely,' Martin said.

There was a moment of collective panic as all of the demons in the room put down the drinks they were holding.

'We can't leave him here like that,' I said. 'He's near the fire. He'll start to … smell.'

Brewster and Cameron took the body away to store in the cellar where it was cold. When they returned, I confronted Brewster.

'So, your master is a killer. This makes you an accessory,' I said.

'He told me this was all just a bit of fun! The guns don't even have any bullets! Me and the missus took this job a few years ago. It's been an easy life. All food and shelter provided for, as well as a good salary.'

'I take it you've never met Mr Black?' I asked.

'No,' said Mrs Brewster, coming in from the kitchen. 'We just work here, and I promise you all, there is nothing dangerous in my food!'

'I have something in my room that will help us test for poison,' Martin said. 'We are stuck here until the boat returns on Sunday, so we'll need to eat and drink before then.'

'I can open a portal to the underground,' Katie Meyers said. 'We can all pass through, and I'll open it up again wherever you wish.'

'I'd rather not,' said Walsh. 'The Sidhe realm might have an impact on my … condition.'

'I doubt any of us would be safe there,' said Grace. 'I had dealings with a Fae once …'

'By that I assume you mean you manipulated one of my kind?' Katie said.

Grace scowled at Katie. Jessica continued to play with the cards on the table between them.

'What are you doing?' Katie asked.

'Reading …'

I was curious to know what our Medusa friend might find in her reading of an ordinary deck of cards.

'I suppose I'll be next?' said Grace.

'No. You won't be,' said Jessica. But she refused to say who would. She gathered up the cards and placed them neatly in a pile.

'If that is all,' said Brewster, 'the missus and me would like to retire for the night. Breakfast will be served in the dining room between eight and ten …'

Brewster bowed to us and walked away in the direction of the kitchen. It was most unusual, considering that a man had just died.

'What? Just like that he's going to bed?' said Walsh.

'I think that's our cue to leave too …' I said to Pepper.

A calm came over them all. A kind of acceptance that the strangeness of the evening was normal.

Perturbed, I said goodnight. There were nine remaining demons. Jessica began to deal a hand of cards again to Grace. Paul Cameron poured himself another brandy.

'I don't poison easy …' he commented.

Walsh sat in the darkest corner of the room, and his body appeared to merge with the shadows as though he were part of them. Katie admired herself in the mirror above the fireplace, as though contemplating her escape portal. Harvey Clark sat in the opposite corner from Walsh. He neither spoke, nor sang, much to everyone's relief. But the Mer studied his shod feet as though they were still a novelty. Then there was Staton. He sat near Jessica and Grace and watched the card play as though it were the most fascinating game he had ever seen. Of all of them, this human judge I understood the least. He wouldn't be the first judge to be corrupt, and I was sure he wouldn't be the last. So why Mr Black had singled him out I couldn't fathom. The story relayed was not uncommon.

Matthewman was the only one of them who acknowledged our departure. He stood by the fire, not far from Katie but keeping his distance from the Fae nonetheless. He nodded his head to me. The fire caught the glow of light burning inside his eyes, marking him as a supernatural creature. I could see the werewolf inside him. Cursed as he was, I doubted that he was evil in himself. He seemed a quiet, unassuming man. Even so, I was relieved that we were not under the influence of a full moon that night.

Then, finally, there was Khan – whom Black had revealed as Captain Nemo. It was no surprise to learn that Khan was a former prince. His bearing was regal. But Nemo or Khan, whatever name he preferred to go by, was indeed a dangerous man. I could feel a raw energy emanating from him. If all that Black had said was true, how might a mortal man change when he spent all of his life underwater and not on land?

Under other circumstances I'd be bringing the house down around all of their ears. But, these were strange times. Even though we'd been invited there and been accused, just like these ten apparent demons, we slayers were not guilty of what Black had said. We killed only when demons interfered with humans. So, what if Black's assessments of the others were wrong also?

We left the drawing room and headed off to our respective rooms. Pepper and Martin did not ask me if I was all right being alone. They knew better than that.

3

The night was uneventful after that. And although I slept with my dagger under my pillow, my sleep was undisturbed.

I woke at 8.00 and by 8.30 I was up and dressed and heading downstairs to join our supernatural companions in the dining-room.

I found Martin and Pepper already there, and some of the people I had now begun to think of as 'demons'.

'Gentlemen and ladies,' Brewster said as he placed a large breakfast platter down in the centre of the table. 'Mrs Brewster's finest breakfast feast.'

The food looked appetising, but none of the demons dug in.

'We all drank rather late,' said Katie in explanation.

'Indeed,' said Brewster. 'Mr Staton is still not up! Mrs B has taken him a tray.'

At that moment there was a loud scream.

Brewster went white and rushed from the room. I followed. The scream had come from upstairs. By the time I reached the landing, Brewster was already there and holding his hysterical wife.

'It's Mr Staton,' he said. 'He's dead.'

I looked into the room and noted that Merv Staton was indeed dead. He lay in his bed. Eyes wide open, lips as blue as Tessier's tongue had been the night before.

Martin arrived and went inside.

'His expression is calm,' he said. 'Looks like he died in his sleep.'

'Poison again?' I asked.

Martin pulled back the covers and there we saw a dagger wound in the middle of Staton's chest.

'This is some kind of game your employer is playing,' I said to Brewster. 'And, if he isn't here, then it means that one of us did this. You two are my biggest suspects right now.'

'But Miss Lightfoot,' said Brewster, 'we are here to serve. Nothing more. These evil doings are a terrible shock to us. Just look at my poor wife!'

Brewster's wife did appear to be in shock. Brewster took her downstairs to their private quarters.

'Where's Pepper?' I asked Martin.

'He remained in the dining-room to prevent any of the others from leaving.'

'Good. Let's take a look around Staton's room and see what we can find.

Brewster returned with Matthewman and they lifted Staton's lifeless body from the bed.

'We'll stow him in the basement with Mr Tessier's body. It's the coldest place in the house,' Brewster said.

Martin and I remained, and then we searched the room.

There was nothing unusual to find among Staton's belongings. Other than the letter that he had apparently received from Mr Black to encourage him to come to the island.

Dear Mr Staton

You are invited to Carnasie Pol, to the home of your business acquaintance Mr Black. Mr Black wishes you to know that it will be worth your while to attend this social gathering of like-minded people.

If you don't attend then you may find the recent loan you took out called in.

Yours

Grace Monroe
Assistant to Mr Black

'Well, at least we know who sent the letters on Black's behalf,' Martin said. 'And that Staton seemed to have little choice whether to attend or not.'

'I suppose Pepper must have got something similar for us?' I said.

'Let's ask him.'

We went downstairs with the letter in hand. In the dining-room the eight remaining demons showed no reaction as we confirmed Staton's death.

'What about the rest of you?' Martin asked, holding up the letter.

When the demons saw it they each withdrew, from pocket or reticule, a similar note. Though they each replaced it before we could read the contents.

'You sent these?' I asked Grace.

'Yes. At Mr Black's request.'

'And how did he make this request?' asked Pepper.

'He sent me a letter. And a list of names. I just wrote to everyone he asked for. And said what he told me to say.'

'Even Pepper? For us?' I asked.

'No. You weren't on my list. But just before I boarded the boat, I received a wire from Mr Black telling me you three were joining us.'

Pepper withdrew his note from his pocket. He held it out to me and I took it. It was very different from that sent to Staton.

Dear Mr Pepper

We've met before. Long ago on an army campsite before a battle that would change the Civil War. A battle I orchestrated.

I knew as I saw you from inside the empty shell of a dead soldier that you would become a great adversary.

It will be worth your while to join me and a few demon friends at a small island I own.

Feel free to bring the delightful Miss Lightfoot and the industrious Mr Crewe. I've been looking forward to meeting them again, ever since they helped you destroy my zonbi horde in New York.

Yours,

Mr Black

'Black is the darkness,' I said. 'It's the only explanation.'

'He's here. He has to be!' said Jessica.

'Keep calm,' Grace said. 'We aren't his enemies. We've always served the darkness.'

'*You* may have …' said Cameron.

'What's … the *darkness*?' asked Matthewman.

'Some say he is a possession demon of great power, others a prince of hell,' explained Cameron. 'But why would he care what crimes we've committed? It doesn't make sense.'

'No, it doesn't,' said Katie. 'And even if he does, he has no say in the Unseelie Court and has no power over the fae.'

Katie approached the dining-room fireplace. There was a large mirror above it with an ornate gold frame. She looked into the mirror – it wasn't the first time that she had admired herself in the glass, either – she had looked very intently at her reflection just a while ago.

'Time for me to leave,' she said.

Then she reached out and touched the glass. The mirror altered, blurring and swirling until it looked like quicksilver. Katie floated upwards toward the mirror, then began to pass through the portal head first. But before her body followed, the portal closed and the mirror re-formed into glass.

Headless, the body dropped to the floor of the dining-room. There was a round red stain on the mirror and smeared over the mantelpiece.

We were now down to seven demons.

4

It was clear that Black meant business. He had no intention of letting anyone escape the island, by normal or supernatural means.

'All we have to do,' Brewster said as he collected the body, this time with the help of Walsh, 'is to sit tight and not do anything stupid until the boat comes back tomorrow.'

'That is,' said Jessica, 'unless Black has cancelled it. He can keep us all here as long as he likes, picking us off one by one.'

'This Black is a demon, you say?' asked Khan.

'Yes,' I said.

'I know him. At least, I've seen him behind the eyes of someone I once knew.'

Six Years Earlier

Prince Ray Khan walked the halls of his palace in some agitation. What was wrong with his mother? She had never been more fractious than she was that day.

'Highness,' said a guard bowing to him as he passed his

father's rooms.

Khan nodded and walked on, heading to the suite next door. He had to talk to her!

Oh, it wasn't just about the engagement. That was expected of him, but this instruction – no, *command* – that he must put aside his passion for invention. It would never do! He was so close to perfecting the engine of the underwater ship. Even marriage could not stop him from completing this work.

Khan didn't know it, but his ability to understand machines was a gift from a higher power: a prayer that his father had made and was answered. It was, they had hoped, a way to arm themselves against the Empire and its oppression. But things had changed since the new arrival of a certain Major in the British army. His parents were now becoming allies with the soldiers. But that didn't mean that Khan had to stop doing what drove him.

'Mother?' he said, knocking on her door. A servant girl answered. Then, bowing, she stepped back and let Khan enter.

'Ray,' his mother said. 'I hope you are ready now to take up your duties and forget this *inventing* obsession. One day you'll be *Mahārāja* and your wife your consort. You must try to make her happy, not spend days on end working on your inventions.'

'I won't give up my dream of making an underwater ship, Mother. I'm so close now. The workings of the engine have fallen into place.'

'I know nothing of what you speak!' his mother said. 'What is *engine*?'

'I'll show you. Tomorrow.'

He left her rooms and went back to his workroom. Inside, the machine he'd created stood on top of a large metal-framed stand, which was reinforced to hold its weight. It was linked to a wheel with huge ridged cogs that were based on those of much smaller clockwork mechanisms. This engine, as Khan called it, was unique though. There had never been anything like it. It would power this magnificent underwater ship that he had already designed. The shell of which had been secretly built some miles away, close to the ocean. Not even his parents knew that Khan had contrived to have the ship prepared already. His mother believed it to be an impossible dream, and his father feared the magic that had given his son such skill – even though it had been what he had wished for.

In the workroom, Khan ordered his workers to move the engine. It was to be sent to the ship that night. He had no intention of showing it to his mother. Instead, he would remove himself to the other location, finish his work and then return in triumph to show them what he'd done.

Once the machine had been moved, Khan gave instructions to his most loyal servants to load some of his personal possessions too. Then, as he was about to leave, his father sent for him.

Unable to avoid it, Khan went to the throne room. There he found both of his parents with the British Major – Black.

His parents sat on their thrones, but when they spoke, it was not their usual voices Khan heard.

'My ssssson …' his mother hissed. 'The Major wants your masssheeen …'

Her body moved unnaturally. She was twitchy and snake-like, and Khan knew that this was not really his mother. Oh, she looked like her, but there was none of the lively mischief he was used to seeing. She looked older, wizened, and the more he studied her, the less like Rashida Khan she appeared.

His father was silent beside her, and when Khan turned

to him, he saw a glimpse of the evil that now inhabited his soul. He'd been consumed by something from the inside. There was, he was sure, nothing of his father there either.

Khan became more aware now of Major Black standing beside him. He looked at the man.

Major Black was a rotund gentleman who had clearly never suffered, as some of his men might have, from rationing. He had the ruddy cheeks of a man who enjoyed his port, and a large handlebar moustache. The man had caught the sun since his arrival, and there was glaring sunburn around the back of his wide neck. But what Khan noticed the most about him was his eyes.

Black's eyes studied him with cold reflection. There was a dull glow within – like the ember of a flame that was not dying, but steadily growing. As Khan looked deeper into those eyes, he felt a painful tug. It was as though some force were trying to rip his heart from his chest.

Khan staggered back and away from Black. He shielded his eyes. Feeling as though they were burning in his sockets.

'You can't run from me forever,' Black said.

But Khan did run. He left his personal belongings, choosing, instead of the howdah-laden elephant, the Major's own horse that was left tethered in the palace courtyard. He leapt onto the back of the animal and rode it hard and fast, as far away as possible.

After a few miles, Khan slowed. He had almost run the horse into the ground in his effort to be away from the palace. His heart had stopped hurting as soon as he had put some distance between him and Black, but Khan was so shaken by the contact that he had forced the horse on regardless. Somehow he understood that Black had tried to consume his soul in the same way he had taken those of his parents.

Slowing now, he saw his servants, sent hours ahead, with his precious machine being pulled along by four stout horses toward its destination.

Khan joined them, and on seeing the normality of his men, began to wonder if he had imagined the whole thing.

Hours later they reached the ocean and the large structure that housed his underwater ship.

Khan wasted no time in having the engine fitted as he stood over the servants, directing their every move.

After that, he instructed them on the interior fixtures, and with the engine in place, the miraculous lighting that channelled through into every area of the ship. This was light captured inside small glass globes. Khan called it electricity, and the use of it was yet another skill he'd discovered after his father's strange wish had brought about the change in him.

'I'll need crew,' Khan said, and among his servants many volunteered.

Then the news arrived …

'Highness,' said one of his servants. 'Rumours come to us of the ill health of the *Mahārāja* and *Maharani*. They say they are letting the British Major rule for them.'

Khan sent a spy back to the kingdom. He was surprised that his parents hadn't sent someone to search for him, and it didn't hurt to have a spy in the midst of this strange invasion by the Empire.

A few days later his servant returned. He was wounded, and had barely made it back from the palace alive.

The *Mahārāja* and *Maharani* were dead, he said. Then the man promptly died himself.

Khan was devastated.

He had the servant's body placed aside and gave instruction to build a funeral pyre to honour him for his loyalty. In lieu of being able to respect his parents in death, Khan intended to give all of his prayers to the funeral of his faithful servant.

A few hours later, though, another creature rose – using his servant's body.

Throwing himself back into his work – an attempt to avoid thinking about his parents' unusual deaths – Khan was alone on the ship. They were close now to risking the vessel's first launch. But he walked around the engine room, studying the temperature and fuel gauges, looking at the mechanism that ran the main engine, and also lubricating the cogs, to ensure that they worked smoothly and silently. The engine was working all the time now to power the ship, and it was proving effective at pumping fresh air in and around the interior, as well as powering the control room and cabins. They had yet to engage the main thrusters that would propel it, as slick as a scimitar, right through the water, but Khan knew the engine would manage it all without difficulty.

Khan planned to launch the next day, and so these final checks were essential, and they took his mind away from thinking about home. Technically he was now the new *Mahārāja*. In a way, he'd already known his parents were gone, the last time he'd seen them. But he desperately avoided thinking about how that had come about. Even his highly intellectual mind could not conceive of how the evil, driven by Black, had consumed the *Mahārāja* and *Maharani*.

He poured some rich olive oil into a cylinder. This was a job his main engine crew would regularly perform, because the engine used lots of the oil when running at capacity. It kept the engine movements smooth and cut down on wear and tear.

'Highnessss …' hissed a voice behind him.

Khan turned, and then he saw his dead servant, dressed now in his funeral robes, standing by the doorway to the engine room.

At first he considered that, tired, he had fallen asleep and was dreaming, but as the creature hobbled toward him, dragging his damaged leg along the floor, Khan knew this was real.

The creature was disintegrating before his eyes.

'I come to deliver a message from Major Black,' he said. 'He's coming for you. He'll suck out your soul. He's already tasted it …'

Khan backed away from the creature, but then he found his back against the machine. The cogs worked silently behind him, the engine purred as it idled.

The advancing creature's eyes glowed; the ember – like Black's – burned brighter as he held Khan's gaze. Khan experienced sharp pain once more in his chest. This time he knew what it was – as Black reached out to him through this walking corpse, trying to capture his soul, he was also trying to take control of Khan's body. Once inside him, the demon would have all the knowledge he needed to use the underwater ship for his own purposes.

As he turned away, trying to fight off Black's power, Khan's hand fell on a length of metal. He pulled it between them, covering his eyes with the glistening metal tube, reflecting the monster's glare back at it. Instantly his strength returned. Then he raised the cylinder and smashed it down on the creature's head.

The man wobbled on his feet, then crumpled. Khan ran outside the ship and yelled for help from his crew.

When they saw the body, some of his men grew fearful and ran away. But Khan's most devoted men picked up the body and hefted it from the ship.

'Burn it,' Khan instructed. '*Without* honours.'

His men hurried to obey.

When Khan had finished his final checks on the vessel, he unveiled the name on its hull.

The *Nautilus* was launched a few hours later.

After that, Khan took his men to the bottom of the sea as though running for his life. He changed his name; no longer would he be known as Khan. Henceforth he would be Captain Nemo.

5

As Khan finished his story, he explained how he preferred to remain in the *Nautilus* near the sea bed.

'You're possibly the only person here who has met Black,' I said.

'I was expecting to see him again. But he's not here,' said Khan.

'Why were you so afraid to be on land?' asked Pepper.

'It is never long before one of Black's creatures finds me. My only safety is below the surface.'

'But why does Black want you so much?' I asked.

'Perhaps because I recognised his control over my parents. Perhaps because I could see that evil light inside him. Or maybe it is because he needs some of the knowledge I have. You see, that day, he took part of me, and now he can find me. I came here to this island by his invitation. I hoped Black would be here, and I could finish him off once and for all.'

'I think you're unfinished business to him too. But answer me this truthfully: was there any credibility to what he said about you on his recording? Have you committed crimes for which you should be punished?'

'I live beyond the law, but I am not a criminal,' Khan said. 'I hurt none. I love the sea and all of its creatures. I am responsible for the deaths of many of Black's monsters, though.'

'I think we three can lay claim to that too,' said Martin.

'Enough of this,' said Cameron. 'There's only a little truth in anything that Black's record said. And that is obviously intended to cast doubt on all of us. I don't see what Khan's story has to do with anything. We are all trapped here. We should be trying to work out how to escape.'

'That's not a problem if Khan has a way to summon his ship,' I said.

Khan nodded. 'You are indeed wise, Miss Lightfoot. I did have a means by which to reach my men. A little device that I invented to communicate with them. However, it was taken from my bag during the transfer from the boat we all arrived on.'

'Look, if what Khan … erm … Nemo … says is true,' Walsh said, 'then Black may have control of any one of us here.'

'Yes,' said Khan. 'Like his servant, Brewster. The man may not even know he's being controlled.'

'Fascinating,' said Pepper. 'Then any one of you is a suspect.'

'Or any of you,' said Jessica. 'And I'm not averse to letting my snakes free at the first sign of any of you turning into one of Black's creatures. I don't care who gets caught in the cross fire.'

'Quite so,' said Harvey Clark, surprising us all that he spoke. 'Black was wrong. I can talk if I need to.'

'What else was he wrong about?' I asked.

Seven Years Earlier

As the Mer staggered on new legs out of the ocean, a song burst from his lips. Then he collapsed, naked and cold, down to the wet sand.

He woke in a human bed. It was not the first he had found himself in over the centuries. The straw mattress pricked his delicate new skin. The air around him hurt, and breathing stung his lungs. The gills behind his ears had stopped working – and he felt oxygen-starved. But he knew this feeling would diminish, just as it had done every time he had been forced onto land.

Clark was grieving. His mate, and her companion, had recently been taken from him, and because the magic that sustained them always failed after seven years, he was forced up onto the land again and again.

Despite his loss, each new return to land was easier than the last. He had learnt much about the world, and this time had chosen to return to Cornwall, in England, to renew his search for one lover who could survive the Atlantic sea with him forever. The search was always the same, but the females were always different.

'You're awake!' said a female voice beside him. She hurried to the door. 'Father! Father!'

The Mer studied the young woman. She was plainer than others he'd come across, and he had developed a certain taste for the beauty of human women. But all that mattered really was that she was untouched by man. For only a pure girl could return to the sea with him.

A man joined her at the door. He was much older, frail-looking even by human standards. He wore black clothing, relieved only by a white collar at his throat.

'I'm Reverend Crosby,' he said. 'And this is my daughter Ursula. What is your name?'

The Mer opened his mouth, and the song poured from his lips. Ursula heard it, and the Mer knew by her responses that she was suitable.

'What a strange tale,' said the Reverend. 'You were accosted. Robbed! How awful! But of course we will help you, Mr Clark.'

From then on they referred to him as Harvey. The story that the Mer told Crosby was one of his own wealth and status. Really, all he did was sing, but Crosby heard the narrative his heart wished for. Ursula heard a different one. She saw him for what he was, but she never revealed it to her pious father. He had kept her close, refusing to let her marry and leave, holding onto her instead for his own selfish desire to have care in his old age.

The reverend's health was not good and Ursula was not a young girl. She had passed 35 on her last birthday and was considered, therefore, to be forever a spinster.

Harvey could change that, though. Ursula heard his song and revelled in it.

But she could not be taken alone. There had to be two. Only one would be his consort, the other would be his consort's companion. It had to be thus, or the women faded faster.

Harvey drew the wealth he needed to him through his song. He sent it out in different directions. A fleet of servants arrived to tend him, a house was offered for his usage nearby. The reverend and his daughter were welcomed into the new social life that Harvey brought with him. And so were all of the local gentry and their daughters.

Harvey found a few impure ones among them, and two possible candidates that lacked the robust nature of Ursula. They were prettier than she, and so he admired and considered them. Ursula remained stoic. She asked him for nothing, and yet he often sought her company.

Then her cousin, Almia, arrived to visit. Harvey's heart was thrown into turmoil. Almia was stunning. A human masterpiece of poise and grace. She was also an innocent. He realised then what it was he saw in Ursula. She was firmly companion material, but when she heard his song, she responded with love, not friendship. This was what was so confusing.

Harvey decided to test them both. From the borrowed manor he called. He sent a song of love and passion: it was Ursula, not Almia, who responded.

Harvey was surprised, but so too was he pleased. Perhaps he, like human men, had been attracted to the wrong females. Maybe Almia and her ilk were not really strong enough to live with a Merman for all eternity, but Ursula might be.

'Almia will be your companion,' he told Ursula. 'Just as you will be mine.'

He sent another song to fetch the other maid, and then the Mer took Ursula's hand and led her down to the water's front. Under his spell she removed her clothing and slipped into the water. She waited, head above the surface, as Almia found her way down the cliff side and to them.

She too removed her clothes, but as she stepped into the water, Harvey realised the mistake he'd made. Almia smelt wrong. She was not under his spell, but rather manipulating it.

'What are you?' he said.

Then he saw a faint, glowing ember in her eyes. It had only recently taken hold of the girl, but the sea would never accept this one. Its taint was a corruption that couldn't be borne.

He sent both women back. Without a companion, he could not take Ursula, and such a companion could now not be found.

Harvey left the Cornish coast and moved inland in his search. It pained him to be so far from the sea, but he had to do this regardless.

Eventually he took two sisters: one younger than the other by a year became his consort, the other joined them as companion. He was happy for a while. But as the usual seven years saw them both fade, and the Mer was forced back up onto land.

As he found a new place to embrace him, he received the letter from Mr Black; and then Harvey Clark travelled across the sea to America to take up the invitation.

6

'But why did you come here?' I asked.

'I never stopped thinking about Ursula,' Harvey explained, his voice soft. 'Black promised to release Almia. Remove his stain from her. I could have them both, and somehow, I knew they'd last ...'

'So your tale is one of love, not of abusing innocent girls?' Pepper said.

'I do ... *love* Ursula,' he said. 'I believe she is my soulmate.'

'Knowing what you are, I have to ask why you haven't just returned to the sea to escape Black's obvious trap,' I said.

'I cannot return without a consort and companion,' Harvey said. 'If I tried, I would drown as surely as a human man would.'

'Fascinating,' I said. 'Just as well that all the ladies here are unsuitable for your companionship.'

'I could send my song out across the bay. There might be a response.'

'What do you mean?' asked Walsh.

'A female or two might appear with a boat by which we could all escape.'

'Then do it at once!' said Walsh.

Harvey was hesitant. 'I can't. If I bond with another two females now, another seven years must pass before I can return. By then, Ursula will be almost 50 in human years. Even now I don't know that she is still the pure girl I cared for. But I still have a chance with her if Black frees Almia. You see, if we are soul mates, she will be able to give me a child …'

'You're saying … the others couldn't?' asked Pepper.

'I've been searching all this time for the *right* one.'

I felt Pepper's eyes on me and met his gaze.

We had to talk about Spain at some time or other, but when our lives were possibly in jeopardy it was not really the right moment. Even so, I knew by his expression that our romance was on his mind too. His eyes had grown softer as he observed me, and I recognised this expression from the very first day we had met.

'By what you have both said,' Martin concluded, 'neither you nor Khan are evil.'

'What of you, Jessica?' I asked. 'What's your story? I assume you have one.'

We had retired to the comfort of the drawing-room now, and Jessica had taken her seat again at the card table. She had shuffled and dealt the cards while Khan and Harvey told their stories, but had made no comment.

Now she put down the deck and looked directly at me. Her icy stare brought a shudder to my spine, but I suppressed it, even though I expected her hair to twist and turn as her snakes freed themselves from her considerable control. She blinked, holding back with some effort. Then the moment passed and her eyes changed.

Fifty Years Earlier

Jessica was born into her condition, as so many demons were, but having been separated from her parents as a baby, she didn't know what she was. She grew up on an island in the Caribbean as the adopted daughter of a missionary and his wife. Her mother had found the child, left at the mission doorstep one morning. Surprised to see a white child left there, and with none of her own, Cynthia Shafer had taken the baby in and raised her as her own.

She had grown up a normal child, and then, one morning, when she woke with stomach cramps, she discovered that she was no longer a child but was growing into a woman.

With menstruation came other changes.

Sometimes when she looked at herself in the mirror she saw those changes, subtle and unique. Her hair seemed to take on a life of its own – twisting and writhing as the strands would somehow clump together.

She dreamed of stone. Statues. Beautiful. Frozen and preserved for all time. A wall of them surrounding her, unmoving. Their presence *fed* her somehow.

Then the Reverend, her adopted father, began to notice her more. Gone was the child, now was the blossoming young woman, who looked nothing like his dreary, work-worn wife, with her red, inflamed insect bites and hatred of the heat they endured as part of their servitude to God.

The Reverend, it seemed, liked his growing adopted daughter. Jessica blossomed and developed, and so did her body, changing shape until it became alluring.

All of the men on the island noticed. Many began to desire her. But as she went about her day in the usual way, Jessica was oblivious of their looks, their lust, their fantasies. She studied with the island children. Listened to the Bible stories read over and over by her mother – she did not know that Cynthia and Arnold were not her real parents and had no reason to suspect.

Then Arnold came into her room one night.

'What is it, Daddy?' she asked.

He stared at her, mesmerised. Jessica became very uncomfortable. Afraid. Under threat. That was when the snakes emerged for the first time.

As the Reverend turned to stone, Jessica screamed.

'*Mummy!*'

Cynthia was roused from a heavy slumber. She ran into her daughter's room, and found the Reverend standing at the foot of the girl's bed.

As she walked around him, she saw the Medusa child for the first time. All of the snakes' eyes were glowing as they turned to her. She was transfixed. She felt the blood freeze in her veins, even as her heart fought to keep the circulation going. It was agony. But Jessica couldn't help it. She killed her mother, feeding on her human energy all the while.

As Arnold's and Cynthia's forms stared back at her, Jessica knew she was somehow responsible. Her body was changing. Her skin glowed with a warmth that she had never experienced before: having always cool skin and cold blood running through her veins. But the energy she'd taken made her feel far more human than she had before. It was then she realised she wasn't human at all.

Her hand went to her writhing hair, even as the snakes shrank back into silken waves. One of them wrapped around her finger; she pulled it forward to examine it, and the glowing eyes winked at her. Then the snake separated into hundreds of strands.

She got out of bed and looked at her parents. They

were fragile. Though stone-like at a distance, close up her they seemed little more than wet sand that had been moulded into her parents' shapes. One snake remained, and it caressed Jessica's cheek. She was unafraid of it, but then, it struck the cheek of her father, and the sharp bite set off a domino effect that made the form crumble. Down it went, slowly disintegrating. The snake struck Cynthia before Jessica could object, and she too fell apart before her eyes.

Jessica felt nothing for them. Her flesh was warm, but her heart was cold. Colder now that she knew she wasn't the same as them, and all of the stories – the religious garbage they had sprouted – meant nothing to her.

The remaining snake whispered to Jessica, telling her who and what she was.

Then the two of them went on a spree.

The island was theirs, and in the end, nothing but stone would remain.

'You have no remorse,' I said.

'It is not in my nature. But over time I have learnt I can control them,' Jessica said. 'Turning people to stone is not always convenient.'

'The snakes are the source of your power,' Pepper said.

'Not a curse?' asked Martin.

'Nothing is a curse unless you make it so,' said Jessica. 'I am what I was born to be. But I don't need to feed them much, and not always with deadly results.'

I didn't ask more. I wasn't sure her story helped us, however. The Medusa I'd met previously had been pure evil. Jessica was cold, and though I couldn't say she was evil, she also had no regrets about the deaths she had caused.

'But what is your connection to Black?' I asked. 'Why did he invite you here?'

'His letter threatened to expose me,' Jessica said. 'It was enough for me to come and try to … take care of him.'

'That doesn't explain his interest in you.'

Jessica shrugged. I knew she wasn't telling me everything. For that reason alone she remained a suspect. After all, her story could just as easily be a red herring, when in reality she was helping Black. If we found out this was true, then I was sure that I would have to destroy her before she could destroy us.

7

There were seven demons left alive at the house. I realised that perhaps I needed to hear *all* of their tales. And so I went to Alan Roman Walsh next. His connection with Black was something that intrigued me.

'I want to hear your story,' I said.

Walsh shrugged. 'I'm not sure I want to tell it. You heard Black's explanation. What more do you need?'

'Your side of it,' said Pepper, 'might help us establish why Black brought you here. With each of us he has an axe to grind. But you, apparently, borrowed money from a Night Shade … So why did he want you here?'

'It wasn't a loan,' said Walsh. 'It was a gambling debt.'

'Go on …' I said.

'And it wasn't the Night Shade I owed money to originally …'

Three Years Earlier

Walsh ended every payday in the Black Sheep tavern. He had a thing for common company; after all, the streets were where he'd started life, and he'd never really shaken his roots. He drank cheap gin with the doxies, buying their time in the hope of sparing them just one John that evening. They were company, and they reminded him of his mother. Walsh didn't know who his father was. His mother had implied it was a gentleman who regularly called. But doxies said things like that to the brats that sprang from their work. Sometimes they said it to the men that were interested in those brats …

Walsh's mother was an honourable woman in her own way, though, as most doxies were. She would never let anyone near her boy. Walsh was the only bastard child she had kept. The others had ended up on the doorstep of the local church or orphanage. All girls. She'd hoped, she told Walsh once, for a better life for her daughters. Walsh knew they wouldn't have had that life had they remained in her care.

As far as Walsh was concerned, Hetty, his mother, did what she could for him. Even managing to put something aside toward his education. And when he was old enough, she'd given him the money, sent him on his way, trusting he'd make something more of himself.

Walsh had.

He'd joined the peelers and worked his way up through the ranks to detective. He had been good at his job. But it had been hard won. And he'd seen his mother, now with a little more disposable income than she'd allowed herself for his sake, finally drink herself into an early grave: just like most of the street girls did.

He regretted not having helped her. For surely Walsh could have, had she waited long enough for him to be in that position.

So – it was a thing he did. Talking to the girls. Paying them for time instead of a bawdy fumble. He also had a taste for gin.

'Eh? Walsh? Want a game 'o cards?' The tavern owner Bill asked. 'They's short a hand in the back.'

Walsh didn't gamble, but he knew how to play, had spent many a winter night with Hetty, or one of her friends, filling time when there were no customers abroad because of the cold. That night most of the doxies were busy and willing to be, the gin sat warm in his stomach and he was bored, so Walsh agreed.

He found he was good at the game – winning most hands and the pot of coins from the centre frequently – and he returned to the tavern more often, reasoning that the money would help the girls. Then there was the night he started losing. The other card players had told him his previous successes were 'beginner's luck', but Walsh had thought he had genuine skill.

He lost more and more, and when he was at the point of deciding the game was not for him, but for fools, his streak changed again, and his pockets were filled once more. The game went in a pattern: sometimes he lost, but overall he was winning. That was until a new player joined them.

His name was Carlson and he was a gentleman. Some said he was a lord. But no-one ever referred to him as anything other than Carlson: as though he had no other name.

Walsh lost heavily in his first game with Carlson, who came out the victor overall. There was the usual chat about beginner's luck, and Carlson's turn for it. No-one was concerned that the man had won so much, for each of the men believed they'd be on a winning streak next.

Walsh's luck changed dramatically for the worse, but by that time he was too sold on the game, and the ebbs and flows of winning and losing, to think about quitting. He continued to lose. Until one day he no longer had any money to offer.

'I'll write an IOU,' Walsh said. 'I'm paid on Friday and can straighten this out then.'

Carlton took the note, but then he sold Walsh's debt on. The man that now owned it was called Mr Black. Walsh didn't know this until Black sent one of his men round to Scotland Yard to see him.

'There'll be interest …' the thug told him.

'How dare you come here!' Walsh said.

The man laughed. 'What you gonna do? Black owns you now. You have a debt to pay. Pay up or it'll be the worse for you.'

The interest was too steep, and so Walsh was left owing something every week. It was a hole he just couldn't seem to get himself out of.

'I've got a friend,' Bill told him at the tavern, 'what can help you out.'

'How?' said Walsh.

'Black's bad news,' Bill said. 'You're a good customer here. I'd hate to see you get in trouble. You need to see Mr Shade. A short-term no-interest loan. Just a one-off payback fee.'

The terms Bill outlined were ideal. Walsh could pay back the loan in instalments, the final one being his one-off fee. No more interest building up meant Walsh could be free of Black.

Bill arranged everything, and Walsh met Mr Shade in the same back room where the card games went on.

'You have six months,' said Shade. He told him the amount he had to pay every week, and Walsh knew it was affordable. Even the final instalment was not beyond his ability to pay. Walsh wondered why more people didn't go to Shade for help.

He bought back his IOU from Black, who tried to sting

him for one final fee. Then Walsh stayed away from the tavern and saved his money, paying the weekly fee off to Shade, while saving up the final £50 for the one-off payment.

But his dealings with Black had changed him. He was no longer the honest detective he had been. Now he turned a blind eye on occasion to some illegal dealings, taking a bribe to add to his pot. Then, on the day the last instalment was due, Walsh returned home to his small flat in Whitechapel, only to find he'd had a break-in. The £50 and a little extra he had saved was gone from its hiding place. Nothing else was touched; it was as though someone had known exactly where to find the money.

But Walsh wasn't too concerned. Mr Shade was reasonable, and he could save up the money again. It was a minor setback.

Walsh met Shade at the tavern. The room was surprisingly dark, and Shade didn't speak, merely held out his hand for the final payment.

'Mr Shade. I have been the unfortunate victim of a crime. The money I had for you was stolen. If you could just give me one more month …'

'A deal is a deal, Detective Walsh,' Shade said.

'But … I was robbed!'

'And now you rob me …?'

Walsh tried to reason with Shade, but all he was told was that he should have read the contract.

'Now you're mine,' Shade said.

Walsh felt ill. His stomach cramped and he doubled over. His legs trembled, barely able to hold him upright, and then Shade told him what he would become and the price he had to pay to hold on to his humanity.

As Shade spoke, Walsh felt his hands and body become so light that a breeze might blow him from one town to the next.

'Remember,' said Shade, 'that you must take the soul of an innocent in order to return to your human form.'

'But why?' Walsh asked.

'To feed me …' said Shade.

Then the Night Shade faded away himself and slipped into the shadows. Walsh was left alone and, when the card players returned to the room, he soon learnt that no-one could see him: he was invisible.

But Walsh could hear everything, and he learnt that the men in the card game were looking for another man to groom for Black and Shade to get their grips into.

The tavern owner Bill aided them, by recommending new players. He brought one to them that night. Walsh saw himself in the naïve young man who joined the table. The man was eager to play, winning every time. It was the start of an obsession that would lead him down a very slippery slope.

Walsh drifted from the room unseen when he had heard enough.

Now he was ethereal he could go anywhere in the tavern, and that was when he found Bill's daughter and her newborn baby.

The baby cried as Walsh approached its cot, but the woman, looking up and peering into the darkness, saw nothing amiss. When the child stopped crying she thought nothing of it. It would be hours before she discovered the newborn was dead.

Armed with an innocent soul, taken through the child's breath, Walsh found himself drawn out of the tavern and down by the Thames. The journey on foot would have taken a normal man at least an hour, but Walsh was there in seconds, and so was the Night Shade.

The Shade pressed its shadowed lips to Walsh's and

sucked the child's spirit from him.

'You've done well,' said Shade. 'And who would have thought what sweet revenge you would get on your betrayer?'

A few hours later Walsh woke in his own bed, fully clothed and corporeal again. He thought the whole experience was a dream; even when he heard of Bill's grandson's cot death.

Then, one month to the day after that, the cramps began again, and Walsh once more became a Shade. He was destined to repeat this monthly thereafter. He was always drawn to an infant, and then would find himself feeding its soul to Mr Shade. After which he'd wake again the next day, fully human.

8

'I have no choice,' said Walsh. 'Surely you can see I am not an evil man?'

'So why did Black bring you here?' Martin asked. 'It seems to me that he has you doing exactly what he, or indeed Shade, want you to do.'

'My note,' Walsh took it from his pocket, 'says he has a way to release me from Shade. That my debt would be paid.'

'But knowing Black as you did, weren't you suspicious of his motives?' I asked.

'I was. But you don't understand. Desperate measures were needed. I've … met someone. I want to have a life of my own. I can't bring her into this awful world I live in. Black's offer was the only chance I had of returning to my old self. Of being able to stop killing innocent children. The only opportunity I have to become human again.'

At that moment Brewster came into the drawing-room.

'We seem to be out of wood for the fire,' he said. 'I'm letting you know because I have to leave the house, to go into the woods to fetch some.'

'I'll help,' said Walsh. 'I need some air.'

'We should all remain together and in the house,' I

pointed out.

Walsh shrugged.

'We won't be long,' Brewster said. 'There's a storm brewing and it gets mighty cold on this island at this time of year.'

Walsh and Brewster left.

I turned back to the room. 'I want to hear from you next, Miss Monroe.'

'I'm not much of a talker,' she said.

'If what Black said about you has any truth, then I need to learn about it. '

'Oh my lord!' came a sudden shouted exclamation from Brewster, out in the grounds.

I ran to the window and looked out in time to see Walsh fading in and out of shadow. He was turning shade.

'But surely he'd known this was near the time of his monthly change?' Pepper said beside me.

Walsh disappeared from view, and we no longer knew where he was.

'I'll deal with this,' said Martin.

Martin went outside. He spoke to Brewster for a while. The man was visibly shaken up by Walsh's sudden disappearance.

I opened the window, and Martin shouted across that he and Brewster would still go and fetch firewood.

'What about Walsh?' Grace asked.

'If what he's told us so far is true, then the shade will guide him to the soul he needs. Then he should be returned to us,' Pepper explained.

I didn't like the sound of that, though I had to accept the reality of it. Walsh would take another child's life to help him regain substance, and there was nothing we could do about it.

Pepper went out to join Brewster and Martin, to take his mind off the inevitable.

'Don't think you'll be getting away with it that easily. Your story please …' I said again to Grace.

But Grace stubbornly refused to talk.

'I'll go next,' said Matthewman.

Sixteen Years Earlier

Steve Matthewman made his way through the woods. He'd taken a shortcut, deviating from the path to a route he knew well. Night was falling and he wanted to reach home before the sun set, and before Farmer Brinkler realised he'd been gone.

Matthewman had taken the job at the farm to help his sister. She was newly widowed, and with one small child and another on the way, was in no position to fend for herself.

Matthewman hated Brinkler. He was an old, bitter man, who beat his wife and children and treated his hired help like slaves. But the pay had helped. After leaving surreptitiously to visit the farmer next door and successfully gaining an offer of better work, Matthewman could now tell Brinkler what he really thought of him. He'd been paid that morning, but planned to disappear again as soon as he told the man he was leaving. Fortunately the farm next door needed help – and Matthewman was pleased to be able to offer something to one of the other men who had a wife and children, and could barely support them on Brinkler's paltry wage.

Heading back to the bunkhouse, Matthewman noted that Brinkler's house lights hadn't yet been lit. Usually his wife had set about making dinner, and the bustle of the farmer's family could be heard. But that night the farm was in total darkness.

Matthewman's curiosity was aroused. Instead of going back to his bunk and retrieving his few belongings, he headed toward the farm house. He was only a few feet away from the building when he realised that something had come out of the forest behind him.

Matthewman turned to see the dark shape of a wolf. He was startled, as this place was not known for the creatures. Even so, he'd heard talk that day of something attacking farm animals in the area. Could this be the culprit?

The wolf had its head down and was sniffing the ground as though tracking something. Matthewman realised it was between him and the bunkhouse. He couldn't get safely inside without the animal seeing him.

Matthewman had nothing to use as a weapon. But he knew that Brinkler kept an axe near the back stoop, ready for his wife to chop up the firewood she needed. Matthewman skirted around the house as silently as he could. But as he reached the back door the wolf was waiting for him.

The creature's eyes held his gaze with an overwhelming intelligence. Matthewman backed away, and the wolf, yellow eyes aflame with hunger, padded toward him.

Matthewman had heard somewhere that wild animals could sense fear, so he tried to steady the harsh beating of his heart.

Before he reached the front of the house once more, he felt another presence behind him. He turned and realised that there was yet another wolf stalking him. This one must be female, he felt, as it was slightly smaller than the one he'd discovered out back.

'Brinkler!' he yelled. 'Bring your shotgun! There are wolves out here, and I'm trapped.'

He backed toward the door of Brinkler's house. Still no light came on, and then Matthewman understood his mistake. Brinkler and his family weren't there. They had gone to town as they always did on the third week of the month. They'd be out buying the month's supply of provisions and would be back late: Brinkler smelling of liquor, his wife smelling of anxiety – for the farmer was always more brutal when he had drink in him.

Keeping his eye on the wolves, Matthewman tried the door of the farm, and to his surprise found it unlocked. He pushed it opened and rushed inside, just as one of the wolves, tired of the game, bounded toward him. He slammed the door shut, but not before the wolf's claws connected with his arm, ripping through his delicate human flesh.

Having drawn blood, the wolf became frenzied with hunger. It reared and threw itself several times at the door. But the door was sturdy, and with the several bolts in place, held out until the animal gave up.

Matthewman was bleeding heavily though. His shirt was ripped and his forearm was gouged. It hurt so much, that he knew some serious damage had been done to him. Damage that might cost him his livelihood, if not his life.

He went into Brinkler's kitchen and found a jug of water, which he used to clean the wound. Then he tore off a strip from his shirt and bound the injury. After that, overcome by blood-loss and exhaustion, he slumped on the ground by the back door and lost consciousness.

A few hours later, Matthewman heard the arrival of Brinkler's carriage, and it roused him. His arm wasn't hurting as much now, and he found he could move it well enough under the bandage. He recalled that he had run the bolts home on the front door. He went over to them and ran them back, then hurriedly escaped the house via the back door. Brinkler wouldn't be happy to find the farm hand inside his home, no matter what the circumstances. Matthewman feared, perhaps irrationally, some accusation.

Matthewman could hear Brinkler's brash shouting as he ordered the children to bed. The farmer slumped down into his chair and let his wife bring in the sacks of provisions alone. Peeping in through the back window, Matthewman could see the wife finding the water he'd used to clean his injury. She frowned, then tipped the jug of tainted water out the back door. Matthewman slunk away, back to the bunkhouse. Inside, the other farm hands were sleeping. They'd all been up before dawn to start another hard day's graft.

In view of his injury, and exhaustion, Matthewman abandoned his plan to confront Brinkler that night, deciding it could wait until morning after all.

He fell onto his bunk and slept.

A month later, working at the new farm, Matthewman had all but forgotten his brush with the wolves, until he heard the sound of them howling in the forest between the two farms. He was happy in his new job. The work was hard, but the pay a little better, and the sweetener was that Farmer Andrew's daughter, Anthea, was pretty and of age. She'd cast her eyes his way, and he was thinking it was time to settle. What better choice than the daughter of a farmer, with a fine dowry? Maybe enough to have their own place?

The farmer had invited him to supper that night. An unusual request, but Matthewman suspected it was because the man saw a good soul in him. And there weren't that many hard-working males that might be suitable enough to wed his daughter.

As he left the workers' bunkhouse, Matthewman looked up at the sky. The moon was so full. It hurt him to look at it. He felt peculiar. His skin itched where the faint scar from the wolf's claw had grown silver and almost disappeared. Matthewman had healed at an amazing rate, but had thought nothing of it beyond how lucky he'd been the night of the attack.

In the forest he heard the wolves again. He could almost understand the meaning of the cry – no, *call*.

His heart was pounding again, but this time not with fear but with a dreadful excitement. Matthewman felt hungry.

He hurried toward the door of Farmer Andrew's house; the moonlight shone down on the path, lighting his way. It hurt his eyes, but his vision seemed to warp and change, dimming as though someone had covered the moon.

There were two steps up to the small porch, and Matthewman tripped up them, as though he had forgotten how to walk on two legs. It was a cold night, but his skin grew hot to the touch. He felt feverish, frantic, aroused – but not in any sense that he recognised.

'Anthea …' he said as he knocked on the door. 'Farmer Andrew …'

His voice sounded odd to his own ears. Distorted and deeper than usual. Then he felt the first shift as his jaw dislocated. He fell to the ground on all fours.

'I'll get it, Father!' he heard Anthea say.

By then he knew that some evil magic had taken him. He tried to shout a warning to her, but all that came from his lips was a deep growl.

The door opened, and he saw his reflection in the eyes of sweet Anthea. Half man, half beast. The girl gasped, too shocked to scream, and suddenly the beast inside him burst forth. *It* knew what to do about the hunger.

Just as the wolf had done to him the month before, Matthewman ripped into Anthea. His claws tore into the girl's throat, cleaving the cry from her. She fell to the floor. Dead. The wolf gnawed on her.

Farmer Andrew stood no chance when the wolf found him in the open kitchen doorway.

After that the wolf worked its way through the household and the farmhands. Nothing appeared to ease its dreadful hunger until every one of them was dead.

The next day, Matthewman woke among the carnage. He saw what remained of his friends and the farmer's family. He had the taste of Anthea still in his mouth. He knew he was responsible. He packed up his meagre belongings and left.

9

'I have had to live with the awful guilt of their deaths,' Matthewman said. 'You cannot imagine what I have endured. Living alone, making sure I am away from humans around the full moon.'

'I understand,' I said. 'By your story, it seems that you were not responsible for what happened. You were tainted by another werewolf, who then abandoned you cruelly to your fate. But what did Black say to persuade you to come here?'

'I ran from the farm and from my friends and family,' Matthewman explained. 'I have never told anyone what I am. I don't think I ever met Black. *But.* He sent me the invitation, and I couldn't refuse ...'

Matthewman took out his letter now. It was still pristine in the original envelope.

Dear Mr Matthewman

I'd like to introduce myself. I'm Armand Black. I know what you are and what you've done. If you don't want yourself to be the subject of a wolf hunt next full moon, then join me at my home on Carnasie Pol.

It will be worth your while, as I may be able to offer you the solution of a cure.

Yours,

Black

'He'd offered a cure, yet still threatened you with exposure …' I said.

'When I had nothing to lose, then the chance of a cure was worth the risk of coming here.'

'Tonight is a full moon,' I said.

'Indeed,' said Matthewman.

Martin and Pepper returned then with their arms full. They dropped the wood into the container by the fire in the drawing-room.

'Any sign of Walsh?' I asked.

The two men shook their head.

It was lunchtime, and Mrs Brewster, though still shaken from finding Mr Staton dead, and from the subsequent death of Katie Meyers, had somehow managed to create a grand buffet for us to eat.

'I'm going to my room,' said Jessica after lunch. 'I suspect we might have to watch out for ourselves tonight. Though, I'm sure I am the only one who has nothing to fear.'

She left the room. Then all of the demons departed one by one. Grace said she needed to go for a walk, and Harvey went with her. Khan said he needed to try to rebuild a communicator, and went off in search of items that might be used. Cameron and Matthewman, being fox and wolf, sat together by the fire in the drawing-room, while I and my companions decided we'd try to talk to Grace again.

We left the house via the front entrance and headed down the steps toward the water's edge.

Grace and Harvey were nowhere to be seen. I shielded my eyes with my hand against the sun's glare as I gazed out over the water.

'What's that?' I said.

Martin peered out over the sea. Then, ever brave, Pepper dived in and swam toward what we realised was a body.

We helped Pepper pull Walsh out of the water. The man was only half himself, however.

'Shark?' I said.

'Not in these waters,' Martin said. 'He's been chopped in half.'

'How?'

'Looks like an axe blow to me,' said Pepper.

'The only axe we had was the one Brewster used for the wood,' I said.

'And Pepper and I were with Brewster when he was using it,' said Martin.

'Not when he first left with Walsh,' I said.

'True, but he was fading at that time. This had to be done when the man was human, not Shade.'

'Then Walsh must also have found an innocent victim.'

'*Help!*'

I turned to see Harvey Clark running toward us. 'It's Miss Monroe …' He stopped when he saw Walsh's body.

'There's nothing we can do for him. What's happened to Grace?' I said.

'She went all Black Widow on me, as soon as we were alone. I suppose she thought that I had a chance of getting her away from here. I … was falling under her spell, and then … from nowhere … bees.'

'Bees?'

'A swarm of them surrounded her, as though she were the honey they needed for their hive. I tried to bat them away from her … much to my own detriment.'

I now noticed that Harvey's arms were covered in stings.

'But why would bees attack for no reason?' said Martin.

'They surrounded her …' Harvey said. 'All stinging at once. She didn't have a chance.'

Grace was not a pretty sight when we found her. Her face and body were covered in stings. She'd half turned into her spider form as some kind of defence mechanism. Now her eight limbs and black body were bloated with bee venom. Around her lay the dead bees, having sacrificed themselves to destroy her. It was a very disturbing sight.

Brewster, Pepper, Cameron and Martin moved her body and Walsh's down into the cellar with the others.

'We're dropping like flies,' said Jessica.

I waited for Pepper and Martin to return from the cellar, and then took them aside. 'Who among the remaining people do you think could have control over the bees?' I asked.

'I wouldn't have thought any,' said Martin.

'Let's look at them all individually. Jessica is a Medusa. If this was a snake attack I'd say she was our culprit. Khan is highly intelligent, but he's human, as far as I can tell. Harvey is a Mer; his powers are useful only in the sea or for luring a mate. Why would he have any control over land insects? Cameron is a Kitsune – have any of us ever known foxes to have any sway over insect nature? And as for Matthewman, he is trying very hard not to excite himself right now. If he wanted to kill anyone, all he need do is allow the change to come. He could slaughter us all in one go.'

'That leaves just Brewster and his wife. They appear to be human, and not involved, beyond working for Black,' Martin said.

'That's if what they said was true. What if Brewster is Black?' said Pepper.

'Maybe it's time we talked to the Brewsters … find out their story …' I said.

10

Brewster was consoling his wife in the kitchen when the three of us found him.

'Right,' said Pepper. 'I want to know how you came to work for Black …'

Cerys Brewster burst into tears at this.

'Go to your room and rest,' Brewster said. 'I'll deal with this.'

Mrs Brewster meekly did as she was told. Glad, I thought, to be away not only from us, but from Brewster himself.

'You'd better tell us what you know, before someone else dies,' I said.

'I don't know anything,' Brewster sighed.

'How did you get the job here?'

'The truth is …' Brewster said. 'I was a deserter.'

'Go on …' I said.

'I got a message that my Cerys was sick. I went to see my commanding officer, but he refused to let me have leave. I was really worried. The letter implied it was serious, and I feared she'd die and I'd never see her again. She's always been fragile.'

'So … you deserted?' Pepper said.

Brewster nodded. 'It was the night before the final push. That last battle ended the war. It was unforgivable in the army's eyes for me to have run from it. When I got home, I learnt Cerys wasn't sick at all. The message I'd received was fake. I couldn't go back, so we tried to lose ourselves in New York. Then I met Miss Monroe, and she hired me for Mr Black. Coming to the island was the best solution. The army would forget about me eventually, and we had comfort, food and money for the days when I no longer had to hide.'

'So, you're telling me you've done nothing wrong?'

'I admit I ran from the war in order to be with my wife. She's my life. I couldn't be without her. Surely you understand that?'

'Black didn't name him on the record, at least,' said Pepper.

I wasn't sure what to make of Brewster's confession, but it did appear plausible, given that Black hadn't necessarily picked people just because they were demons. There was nothing supernatural about Brewster, or my cat senses would have revealed it by now. If anything, his worry for his wife's health showed him to be a caring and loving husband. Certainly not someone worthy of Black's attention at all. In which case, why would Black even *help* Brewster?

'If you don't mind, I'd like to make sure Cerys is okay,' said Brewster.

We didn't stop him leaving.

'I'm going to look for Mr Khan and see how he is doing with that communication device. Perhaps I can help him,' said Martin.

He left the kitchen, closing the door behind him.

I found myself alone with Pepper.

'So, what do you think is going on here?' he said, after a

pause.

'Black has an axe to grind with us all and he's going to try to kill us all off?' I said, stating the obvious.

'I meant … with us?'

'*Oh*! Pepper … We both know exactly what is between *us*. We're both good at ignoring it though, aren't we?'

'Is it your desire to continue to ignore how we obviously feel?'

I thought for a moment, not sure what answer Pepper really wanted to hear. Was it easier to ignore it until we were out of this danger, knowing full well we'd be in another spot before long?

'There'll always be another demon …' Pepper said, as though reading my thoughts. Then he pulled me to him and kissed me.

For once I didn't pull away first, he did.

'I'm sorry, I should have asked you first …' he said.

I leaned into him and offered my lips again. Pepper took them. And I lost myself in his embrace, pushing away all thoughts of demons and Mr Black.

'I'm sssorry to disssturb you,' said a voice behind us.

Pepper and I parted and turned to see the Great Inspiro standing by the cellar door.

'Good grief! We thought you were dead, man!' said Pepper. Then Inspiro lumbered out and toward us, and we both realised that he was indeed dead, and very hungry.

I bent down and pulled my laser pistol from my boot, even as Pepper unsheathed the sword from his walking-stick.

Brewster opened the door from the servants' quarters. He staggered back in shock, unseen by the *zonbi*. Meanwhile, Inspiro, aka Tessier, moved farther into the kitchen, with the gait of the newly dead. *Rigor mortis* was still affecting his limbs, and he walked stiff-legged and stiff-armed toward me.

'You are sssuch a tasssty morsel, Miss Lightfoot. And I'm hungry enough to forget my human originsss and treat you and Mr Pepper as the cattle you are meant to be …'

'Stay back, Tessier, if you know what's good for you,' Pepper said. He gallantly stepped in front of me then, blocking me from Tessier's vision.

Tessier turned his eyes to Pepper – his death-whitened irises gave him the appearance of a blind man – and licked his decaying lips. An ink-black ichor dripped from his tongue. His smile was lascivious as he revealed a mouth full of rotten, poisonous teeth.

'I'll enjoy infecting *you* firssst …' he said.

Pepper raised his lethal sword in front of him, ready to swing – and I'd seen him use it many times effectively against the undead – but before he could move, Tessier made a sudden lunge toward us.

Blood and brains splattered on the walls of the kitchen as Tessier's head exploded. The undead creature crumpled at the knees and pitched forward, landing face down just one step away from Pepper's feet. Behind him we saw Brewster, holding the strange pistol that Black had given him.

'The … darkness …' Brewster stuttered.

'You've seen these things before?' said Pepper.

'In the camp … three years ago.'

Then he told us an all too familiar tale of how the *zonbi* epidemic had spread through his camp, affecting soldiers of both low and high rank indiscriminately – and why he had really deserted his post.

After he had finished his story, none of which came as any surprise, as Pepper had been through a similar experience himself, Brewster then revealed the real reason he worked for Black.

'Me and Cerys were hiding out. Her cousin had a farm, and we went there as workers using a different name. Things were fine for the first two years, but then, about a year ago, Black sent me a letter. In it he said he *knew* who I really was, and what I'd done. He offered me the job here, with a promise to maintain his silence about my whereabouts. It was implied that refusal would result in the army learning exactly where we were.'

'Why would Black care about your desertion?' I asked.

'When I went to see my commander,' interjected Pepper, 'I looked into his eyes, and I saw the darkness. I escaped it. And so did Brewster. What we all failed to realise was, the darkness saw us too, and it wasn't going to let us go that easily.'

Brewster's hand was trembling as he placed the gun onto the kitchen table.

'I didn't know … not until things started happening, that Black was … *is* the darkness,' said Brewster. 'I never even suspected. We've been treated well since we arrived here. You've got to believe me: I just thought that Black was looking for employees who had too much at stake to leave. He wouldn't be the first gentlemen who enjoyed having something over the servants.'

'Mr Brewster,' I said. 'If we are going to get out of here, then we all have to work together. How do you get word to Captain Carey to come and bring provisions?'

'The lighthouse …' said Brewster. 'I send him a signal.'

'Then let's go there and do that, shall we?' said Pepper.

'What about Tessier's body?' said Brewster.

'We'll need to burn it,' I said. 'Just to make sure he can't be used again. And the other bodies too.'

11

'Where's Staton?' said Cameron.

It was then we noticed that Merv Staton's body was no longer in the cellar, though Walsh, Grace and Katie were still there. Martin, Cameron, Matthewman and Khan brought the four corpses out and piled them high on a funeral pyre that Jessica and I made. Harvey kept back from the flames but watched as the kindling was lit, with the fascination of someone who had rarely seen fire.

The bodies were dry and ripe for burning, and the smell of roasted flesh sickened the air, along with the rotted, *zonbi* smell that came from Tessier's body as the flames danced over him. I heard the sizzle of the black slime that ran in his veins now instead of blood – it was quite combustible – as it went up in a whoosh.

When the bodies were burning well Brewster and Pepper went to the lighthouse to send a message to Carey. But part of me knew already that this was a useless exercise. It was unlikely that Carey would come; Black would no doubt have already given him instruction to ignore all messages from the island. Even so, I didn't voice these concerns, or spread doubt on Brewster's surety that Carey would come to the rescue. The man needed hope, as we all did, and I wanted to let myself believe that Carey would do the right thing and return.

With the revelation of Brewster's real story I was beginning to wonder if the others had told us the truth also. I'd heard all of their explanations except, I realised, that of the Kitsune, Cameron.

As the bodies were consumed, I pulled the man aside and asked him to tell me his story.

'I want the truth, Cameron. Otherwise there is nothing I can do to help you.'

Cameron nodded. 'I'm willing to talk to you. But not here. The stench … sickens me.'

Kitsunes, like all foxes, had sensitive noses, and I was sure that the odour, which I could barely tolerate, was far worse for him.

We went back into the house and took a seat in the parlour. I watched Cameron's face as a range of emotions ran over his features.

'A girl *did* die in my care. But I didn't know about it,' he said. 'Black lied about that. Or didn't have his facts straight.'

'Who was she?' I asked.

'An innocent. Probably tainted by the darkness. Though I was unaware to what extent. You see, I didn't really know her, or much about her. I knew her brother though … *Intimately* …'

Eight Months Earlier.

'I can only prescribe this for a short time,' Paul Cameron said. 'Laudanum is highly addictive. After that, your sister will have to learn to face the reality of your parents' death.'

'She needs to rest right now. Build up her strength. To see the servants turn … *feral* … like that. They tore my mother apart before Tatiana's eyes,' said Stefan. Then he buried his face in his hands, rubbing at his eyes as though this could remove from his mind the awful imagery.

'There have been some strange things happening recently. Your parents were not the first to be attacked by … an *insane* mob,' Cameron said.

Stefan looked up. He met Cameron's eyes and saw only sympathy and understanding. 'If it hadn't been for my arrival,' he told him, 'Tatiana would be gone also. Those monsters … *ate* my father … Tatiana locked herself in the kitchen. I had been out hunting and had my rifle. I put them down like the rabid dogs they were.'

Cameron took Stefan's hand in his. 'You shouldn't have had to see that either. How are *you* coping?'

'At least I had the benefit of instant retribution,' Stefan said.

Stefan took back his hand. But Cameron had noted the tremble, and knew it wasn't just from the shock of what Stefan and his sister had endured, but also from the rush of emotions he had for the Kitsune. Emotions he had to come to terms with: for Victorian polite society did not welcome men who were lovers of other men. Even so, Cameron knew Stefan would get over his fear eventually, if he loved deeply enough. Then Cameron would be happy to introduce him to all that his devotion could offer in return.

Stefan pushed the medicine bottle into his pocket.

'Thank you for this. I didn't know what else to do.'

'Just two drops a night,' Cameron said. 'And only for a week or two. Until she begins to calm down. Until she can begin to accept what happened.'

'How can any of us accept *this*?' Stefan said.

Cameron knew that Tatiana was not the kind of young woman who found hardship easy. Her father was an English lord who had married a Russian aristocrat's daughter. Tatiana was as highly strung as her mother had been, whereas Stefan had the calm Englishness of their father.

'Sleep is undoubtedly the best cure for everything that ails the mind,' he said. 'Be assured she will recover. You both will.'

Stefan left then, and Cameron didn't see him for a week, by which point he had changed from a desperate, frightened man to a confident and outgoing soul once more.

'I have to thank you,' Stefan said. 'My sister is transformed!'

'That's good news,' Cameron said. 'Now, reduce the dose to one drop a night, and then next week stop the usage altogether.'

Stefan nodded and agreed, and then he hugged Cameron awkwardly. When they parted, Cameron placed a kiss on his cheek.

'It will all be fine. There's nothing to fear.'

'Thank you, Paul. For everything,' Stefan said again. He hugged him once more, and that was the last time Cameron saw him.

A few weeks later, Cameron heard that Stefan had sold their family home, and that he and Tatiana had moved away. He was shocked by the news, because he had really thought Stefan was beginning to have feelings for him. He was even more surprised that Stefan hadn't told him he was leaving London.

He sent word to his lawyer, Mark Philips, to find out where Stefan and Tatiana had gone. The news that came back confused the Kitsune even more.

'After liquidating all of their assets, he left alone,' said Philips.

'I don't understand. His sister was joint beneficiary of their father's estate … where is she?' Cameron said.

'I'll search further. I have some informants who may be able to help …' said Philips.

Cameron paid him and then, as he left, decided to go in search of some information himself.

It was risky, but he went to the underground. There he was greeted by a fae that Cameron knew bestowed favours for a price. The fae was over six foot five tall, with white blond hair, a beautiful man by any standards. Even Cameron, with his own supernatural abilities, found the fae's green eyes compelling.

'What is your desire?' the fae asked.

'I need to find Lord Stefan Rowley,' Cameron said. 'And his sister Tatiana.'

'I can help you. But there will be a price,' the fae said.

'Name your price, and then I might agree,' said Cameron.

'You *will* agree,' said the fae. 'In a few months' time a young woman called Katherine Lightfoot will come into your life. You will bring her to us. For this I give you Stefan and Tatiana.'

'Why do you want this woman?'

The fae smiled. 'My queen wishes to speak with her. Nothing more.'

Cameron agreed to their terms, for he saw no harm in obliging the fae. This was something he could offer, that they, for some reason, could not obtain for themselves.

'Where is Stefan?' Cameron asked now.

The fae looked away from Cameron, out over the rolling hills of the underground, as though his ethereal gaze were searching out the answers.

'Stefan is in Russia. Tatiana is closer to home.'

'Why didn't she go with him?' Cameron said.

'She was unable to go.'

Cameron frowned. For all that he had struck a deal, the fae still fed him ambiguity.

'Where is Tatiana? Will she have answers for me?'

The fae nodded. 'When you find her, your real question will be answered.'

'My real question?' Cameron said.

'Not where Stefan is, but *what* he is?'

The fae dismissed Cameron then. Telling him to 'search closer'.

Cameron returned to his apothecary shop in Whitechapel. He had left it closed for an entire day while he traversed the underground, and another while he found his way back to the human world. He had been careful not to eat or drink there, and now his hunger and thirst reared their heads.

Inside the shop he found several notes that had been posted by his regular customers who wanted medicines. He placed these on the sales counter, planning to process them and send the medicines by trusted urchins.

But first, Cameron needed a drink. Downstairs in his cellar he had some saki. The Kitsune rarely drank alcohol, but this was an occasion when he felt the need to calm his nerves. Dealing with the fae was always intimidating, and he hoped he would never have occasion to visit the underground again. The place, though incredibly beautiful on the surface, was ugly underneath. The courts of Seelie and Unseelie were often in feud, full of intrigue and betrayal. Cameron knew that no 'agreement' made was ever fair or just. But down there, listening to the green-eyed fae, he had been unable to resist the request, and the deal had been made. He would not dare to fail to deliver on his side of the bargain. But what had the fae really given him? A riddle. Tatiana was close to home, but Stefan had gone to Russia. Cameron found this hard to understand. Out of the two siblings, hadn't Tatiana been the one most likely to go to the land of their mother? Hadn't Stefan always been so proper? So … English?

Cameron opened a door off the small shop and, carrying a lantern, walked down the steps into his cellar.

Among the jars and unguents, the dragon's breath, mandrake root and other rare ingredients, Cameron's stash of saki was in a small crate. He pulled out one of the bottles, uncorked it and took a deep swig of the liquid.

At that moment he dropped his Englishman façade and became the Japanese fox-like man. Shirking his glamour was like scratching an irritating itch.

In his real persona Cameron's fox senses were also heightened. It was then he became aware of the opiate.

Thinking that one of his servants had secretly been indulging in a dragon chase, he moved through the cellar to his other store room.

This room was set out for those rare occasions when Cameron treated someone with a mental disorder. The opiate helped him reach the inner mind of the sufferer, relaxing and opening him or her up to suggestion. Through hypnosis, Cameron had helped to recover many a mind thought to be truly lost.

But such treatments were rare, and Cameron had not delivered one for a long time. More than a year. He could not explain, therefore, the lingering odour of opium.

He pushed open the door and found the room filled with smoke. His sensitive nostrils tingled, and he wrapped his fur-covered paw over his nose to avoid inhaling the drug.

Moving through the room, Cameron went to the cellar

doors above, and throwing them open, vented the smoke out into the London smog. He knew it was unlikely that anyone would notice extra fog in this vile miasma.

When he turned back to the room, the haze was clearing, having been sucked out into the cold air above.

Then he saw her. A wasted, skeletal thing, barely alive.

He hurried to her side. He hadn't met her before, but Cameron knew that this poor child was none other than Tatiana Rowley.

As he began his examination to assess her condition, Tatiana breathed her last. Cameron was overwhelmed. Confusion. Fear. Even remorse. How had she come to be here without him even being aware if it? Who had given her the opiate and then callously left her unattended?

He was mortified.

As Cameron finished telling me his tale I took in the implications of all he had said.

'I realised that Stefan had to be behind the death of his sister. But I didn't know how he'd done it.'

'The last time you saw him, you said he appeared changed?'

'Less anxious. Better.'

'There is obviously a very simple explanation,' I said. 'That is he stole his sister's inheritance and killed her for it.'

Cameron squeezed his eyes shut. For a moment the Kitsune fox appeared over his features, but it was gone in the blink of an eye. Cameron was strong. His magic, even when he was suffering intense emotional pain, was always under his control.

'I know what you say is true. But it is difficult for me to accept such cruel behaviour.'

'Humans can be very brutal, and greed is a huge part of why they are capable of committing terrible crimes against each other.'

'I looked further into his affairs after this,' Cameron said. 'I learnt that Stefan gambled. He was a womaniser too, and so his overtures to me had all been … *fake*.'

'I'm sorry,' I said. 'It appears that he manipulated you all along. I have to ask you … why did Black invite you? And, why did you accept?'

'He told me Stefan would be here. I believed it. I wanted …'

'Revenge?'

'I don't know. Part of me just wanted to confront him. Learn the truth. Was he involved with Tatiana's death? Or was he made to look guilty. I'd have to look into his eyes and ask those questions, then I might learn who and what he is.'

'I do have one more question,' I said.

'Of course.'

'How do you propose to convince me to go to the underground with you?'

'I don't,' said Cameron. 'I never had any intention of fulfilling my bargain with the fae once I met you.'

'Then … you will be opening yourself up to a whole load of pain. They won't let you get away with it, Mr Cameron.'

'I know,' said Cameron. 'But I couldn't ever be responsible for putting you in harm's way, Miss Lightfoot.'

12

I left Cameron in the parlour and went back outside to see the funeral pyre falling into ashes.

'The threat is gone,' said Jessica.

'I don't believe it is,' said Pepper.

'Where's Brewster?' I asked.

'He's missing. As is Mrs Brewster. I left him at the lighthouse sending the signal to Carey. When I returned he was gone. After that I went to his quarters. The pair of them had packed and left.'

'But how can they? There's only one way on and off the island,' I said.

'Well, that's what we were told,' said Pepper. 'But maybe Brewster had a way out all along.'

'So Brewster has been lying to us?'

'Brewster may be Black for all we know. After all, he was here when we arrived. He's the one that was holding the pistols to force us to listen to the gramophone.'

'He did kill Tessier though. We were almost *zonbi* lunch,' I said.

'True, but that could have been part of his plan. After all, where is Staton's body?'

I was starting to get a headache, and my fangs itched in

my gums – a condition that was occurring more frequently these days whenever I became agitated. It went along with the urge to bite and scratch people. Either a cat or a vampire urge, I wasn't sure which. Black was right about that at least. I really didn't know what I was anymore.

I filled Pepper in about Cameron and the fae's apparent interest in me.

'Do you believe him?' Pepper asked.

'About as much as I believe anyone on this island that's not one of our team,' I said. 'He might be telling the truth. He was sincere. But, the darkness is clever, and he could be manipulating Cameron to appear trustworthy. A bit like Brewster I suppose.'

Pepper nodded. Then, despite the fact that Jessica and Harvey were with us, he embraced me.

'I wondered about you two,' Harvey said. 'I guess I don't need to wonder anymore.'

'She's not available as Mer-mate,' said Martin, walking toward us. 'That's for certain.'

Harvey glanced at me and then Jessica. 'Both these ladies could be suitable.'

I saw Jessica's hair twist and writhe, but she ran a hand over the strands, smoothing it down before it could form into the lethal snakes.

'I'm not sea fodder either, Mr Clark,' she said. 'But you are right in your assumption that I have never loved. In my condition such a commitment could be disastrous to any potential lover. My snakes are jealous creatures …'

I did not ask where she thought she had originated from. For surely her appearance as a baby would suggest she had been born, and some kind of union had occurred between a medusa and a male.

I didn't admit my purity to Harvey, but I felt Martin's

eyes on me, curious, because he knew that Pepper and I had shared a room before. Playing husband and wife came naturally to us, but Pepper was always respectful, no matter what. What happened behind closed doors with us would always remain between us, though.

I pulled away from Pepper's embrace as the wind picked up and began to blow around the remnants of the pyre.

'We should give them to the water,' suggested Khan. 'It is the only dignity they have left.'

Then Khan began to sweep the ash over the rocks and drop them down into the water below.

Matthewman went to help, and soon the dead were scattered into the water, to be carried away on the current.

Matthewman stood at the edge of the cliff, looking out over the sea as the sun began its descent. As Brewster had warned, a storm was building, and thick clouds now drifted over the sky.

I couldn't see the moon as it rose, but I should have realised that Matthewman would at least be able to feel it. Perhaps I hoped he could hold back the change longer. But that was naïve of me, having never dealt with a werewolf before.

His skin began to glow and he threw out his arms as though he expected the wind to lift him up in the air.

'Run ...' he roared as he fell forward onto all fours. 'Can't hold ... back.'

White fur rippled from his head and spread to the rest of his body. There was a loud, painful cracking sound as bones shifted. Matthewman's face elongated and re-formed.

I didn't want to leave him in the throes of his change, but Pepper was my voice of reason:

'If we stay, we'll have to kill him, Kat. Better to let him

change and roam the island until morning.'

Khan, Harvey, Martin, Pepper and I hurried back to the house. Only when we were inside did I realise that Jessica had remained behind.

'We have to get her in here,' I said.

Clark shook his head. 'He won't kill her. She'll turn him to stone first.'

'I don't want either of them to die,' I said.

I hurried to the window and looked out, and there I saw Matthewman, fully changed, embracing Jessica as though she was his long lost love. But the expression on Jessica's face said otherwise: Matthewman was crushing her, and as she died, the snakes burst from her head and turned their deadly glare on the wolfman. He froze. Matthewman's long white fur stopped flowing in the wind. It solidified, turning whiter still, and then the beast's arms stopped squeezing. He was a statue before Jessica took her last breath. The snakes shrivelled back into her head. Her hair changed colour, turning as white as Matthewman's fur, and then the Medusa too turned to stone. Her final act had been to become what she created.

'They're dead,' I said, as Pepper joined me by the window.

'Look!' said Martin.

I turned back to look at the conjoined statue and saw the remains of one final, still mobile snake strike Matthewman's cheek. The werewolf crumbled to dust, and then the snake struck Jessica. A final bite that killed its host, as well as ending the life of the snake itself. The snake dropped and disintegrated as Jessica's body fell apart and turned to dust.

'My god!' said Pepper. 'Why did the snake turn on her?'

'She was already dying. Matthewman had crushed her

in his powerful arms. The snake just … put her out of her misery and pain,' I explained.

The wind picked up again outside, and without our help it blew the remnants of the werewolf and the medusa toward the cliff-face. I watched as the dust danced over the edge and into the sea.

'Where's that coming from?' I wondered.

But as I turned I saw the answer: Harvey's lips were pursed as though he made a silent whistle.

'You can control the wind?' Pepper said.

Harvey stopped moving his mouth and the wind fell back. 'This close to the sea it's possible for me. I need to return to the sea soon. But the only way I can do that is to lift the taint from my soulmate's companion. If Black doesn't reveal himself soon, then I don't know how we will ever be able to do that.'

I didn't say anything, because I couldn't imagine how such a thing could ever be possible, despite Black's promise. Once a soul had been touched by the darkness, how could it ever be pure again?'

'We ought to go and make sure the ashes are all gone, and the stone dust,' said Martin.

I glanced back out of the window, noting the remains were indeed all gone, but didn't comment. I understood how Martin was feeling. He had to have closure on these two – we all did.

So it was with much slower progress that Khan, Harvey, Martin, Pepper and I all went outside again. We stood on the spot where the medusa and the wolf had held a final, brief embrace. I wondered if it was suicide for them both, or just for Jessica. Surely she had known she couldn't win if Matthewman got her in his grasp?

A pale purple flower was blossoming on the edge of the cliff-face. I picked it and placed it down on the spot where they had both died.

We were down to three demons. If indeed these men could still be called that.

I looked out over the sea. The storm that had threatened had blown away with Harvey's sea breeze. The tide was coming in, and across the bay I thought I saw a boat slowly moving toward the island.

'Martin! Pepper! Look!'

'Good God! Brewster must have sent the SOS after all!' said Pepper. 'Carey's coming!'

'Let's get down there and get off this island,' said Khan. 'I can contact my ship once on the mainland.'

'Mr Cameron is still inside,' I said. 'I'll go and tell him Carey's coming.'

Clark, Khan, Martin and Pepper went down to the jetty to wait for Carey while I returned to the house to talk to Cameron. I went into the parlour but there was no sign of him.

In the hallway I called his name but received no response. I went into the kitchen to search for him, thinking that perhaps he had gone to look for sustenance, but there was no sign of him there.

Then I heard a noise coming from the quarters of Brewster and his wife. I withdrew my diamond shard blade from my boot, and retrieved my laser gun for good measure. Realising that pretence at respectability was probably pointless now, I removed the skirt, revealing my britches beneath. I now had full access to all of my weapons.

I opened the door to Brewster's quarters and followed a short corridor down to the couple's room.

The door was ajar, so I wasted no time in pushing it open.

Merv Staton had Brewster's guns and was holding

Cameron at bay with them.

I raised my laser weapon and pointed it at Merv, though I didn't shoot. He didn't look dead, or a *zonbi*, and I thought I ought to discover exactly what he was before I fired.

'Ah, Miss Lightfoot,' he said, flicking his eyes briefly my way. 'You've interrupted my exchange with Mr Cameron.'

I looked into Staton's eyes, and then I knew exactly who he was. Who he had been all along.

'Mr Black, I presume?' I said.

'You always were intelligent,' he said. 'Of course, I've enjoyed playing with you and your colleagues all this time. I shall miss you.'

'There's no need,' I said. 'I'm not going anywhere.'

'Miss Lightfoot, you must realise this is the end of your brief, but exciting, rebellion. When you and your colleagues are gone, there will be no resistance as my kind sweep over the world.'

'You have grand designs, Mr Black. But that is assuming that you can kill me and my colleagues. You'll find us quite resourceful.'

A large explosion shook the house. I lost my footing and almost let go of my weapons, but my reflexes were good, and though I stumbled I quickly regained my balance.

'What was that?' asked Cameron.

I was halfway in the room when he turned to look at me, full Kitsune and no sign of his English gentleman glamour. Cameron was scared.

'That,' said Staton, 'was Captain Carey's boat exploding. I suspect all were aboard and will go down with it.'

My first thought was of Pepper and Martin, but then I

wondered about Khan and Harvey – both from the sea in their different ways. Were they now permanently a part of it?

My heart slowed down as my cat-vampire instincts kicked in.

'If they're dead you'll soon follow, Staton or Black or whoever you are.'

'You have often referred to me as the darkness,' Staton said. 'I rather like that name.'

I saw that ember inside his eyes begin to glow, vibrant but cold. An icy flame that came not from fire but from something else entirely. The darkness was the only name you could give this evil entity. Seeing that spark grow was terrifying, but my heart slowed further and I kept my fear in check. The predator in me rose to the surface. My blood ran cold, and all emotion left me. My vision changed, sharpened, and so did my senses.

I heard Cameron's whiskers twitch as I drew closer to him. Maybe my scent changed too when my hybrid rose, because I was sure he smelt my fragrance in the way that animals explore other animals in order to determine if they are friend or foe. Right then I was neither, because I didn't trust Cameron any more than I trusted Staton.

Staton turned the pistols toward me.

'I would enjoy *eating* you, Miss Lightfoot. The darkness is always hungry, but I fear the blood inside you may be poison to me. And so your death must be a very dull one instead.'

A split second before he fired, the room lit up with an extraordinary light. Cameron grabbed my arm and yanked me toward it. He was stronger than expected, and I found myself unable to resist. I didn't even have time to register what was happening, before Cameron pulled me through the tall mirror on Mrs Brewster's wardrobe.

I heard gunfire behind me, then the light went to black and I was stumbling around in a tunnel.

'Forgive me,' Cameron said at my side. 'I had to do it. There was no choice. Staton would have killed you.'

'What have you done? Where are we?'

'The underground,' Cameron said. 'I always had an infallible escape route. The fae … the one who told me about Stefan. He gave me this.'

Cameron raised his hand and showed me a small glowing orb. It gave off enough light to show us we were in a dark tunnel; one under a forest, judging by the twist of tree roots that lined the earthy walls.

'The orb was activated when we were close enough to each other. I took the chance.'

'I have to get back. Reverse it. I'll kill that …'

'I can't reverse it,' Cameron said. 'It was a one-way ticket, and our only return will be if, and when, the fae give us passage out.'

'But Pepper and Martin?' I said. 'They could be hurt.'

'They could be dead,' said Cameron. 'But there's nothing any of us can do now.'

Ahead a light began to glow, and Cameron's orb turned blue in his hands as though responding to some other message.

'We have to follow it. Look, all he said was that his queen wanted to speak to you. We can go and do this, and maybe they'll help us to return.'

I sighed, but my heart rate was still in battle mode, so I felt no fear, just agitation. I had been close enough to Staton to reach him had I wanted to. My chance of killing him had been taken away from me and now I didn't even know if my friends were safe.

We emerged from the tunnel into a huge chamber. In the centre was a table heaving with food and jugs of wine and ale.

'Don't touch it; it's a common fae trick,' said Cameron.

'I know.'

We passed the food and left the chamber. Here was a fairground with rides devoid of people but still moving. As we reached the first one, a carousel, it stopped and the gate to the safety fence opened. I saw then a barker, and he beckoned us through. I felt the tug of attraction to the ride, but Cameron gripped my arm and pulled me past.

The gate closed as we went by, but other rides stopped, and the same barker tried to tempt us to take part.

'Once you go on board, you can't get off,' said Cameron.

I looked back at the carousel and saw it was full of people riding round and round; some looked terrified, others bemused.

'The fae keep us here by making us forget who we really are. All those unfortunate souls are suffering, but don't know why.'

'What do the fae gain from this?' I asked.

'Entertainment. What else?'

I knew the fae were selfish and cruel. Hadn't I met them once before? Hadn't one of them enjoyed kidnapping young girls from the school where I'd posed as a teacher? But the more I was in this world, the further away my own was. I suffered some form of displacement. I was both a part of and separate from this place, and the two conflicting emotions confused and concerned me. I had never felt like this before. Except perhaps when I was a child.

'Talk to me,' said Cameron. 'Tell me what memory they have asserted in your mind.'

'Memory?'

'Yes. A false memory, probably.'

'My childhood,' I said. 'I remember feeling different then.'

'Mmm,' said Cameron. 'That's a possible truth. Because you have always been different, Miss Lightfoot.'

'A fae helped me pass through here once. He might again,' I said.

'Don't speak of it. Trees have ears.'

We were walking through a forest now, and it felt like midnight, but I recalled how odd the times were in this fae land. How one minute it could be dark, the next light.

'Do you know where we are?' I said.

'We've just left the Unseelie realm. We are being summoned to the Seelie court.'

'The *new* Seelie queen wishes to see me then?'

'New?' said Cameron.

'Yes. Aleora was imprisoned and a successor to the throne was appointed.'

'Oh dear,' said Cameron. 'You've met Aleora before?'

I saw Cameron's Kitsune fur ripple in agitation and was surprised that such a thing could occur in a fox's expression.

'What is it?' I said.

'You don't understand. In the future Seelie court, Aleora *is* dethroned.'

'What do you mean, *future*? That was a few years ago.'

'Time doesn't work the same in the underground as it does in our world. Time is relative not to when it is for us, but when and where we enter the realm. This orb has brought us to a specific time and place. This time is the reign of Aleora.'

'How do you know?' I asked.

'Feeling time is one of my gifts,' said Cameron.

A large white, glowing gate stood open ahead of us, like the gates of St Peter waiting for the deserving to enter heaven.

'The Seelie court … and the open gate is a welcome sign for us.'

'I'm sure it is,' I said. What did Aleora want from me? Did she know that I would be her future downfall?

'Whatever you do,' said Cameron, 'don't talk about meeting her before. Don't tell her anything about her future.'

It was sound advice, for if she knew, then surely the future could be changed. My head began to hurt again as I explored the possibilities of time and the confusion of my past with her present.

'Try not to think too hard on it,' Cameron said. 'Just know this: the queen's future cannot be changed, because it is already in *your* past.'

We passed through the Seelie court gates, and then we heard a fanfare of angelic trumpets.

'She knows we are here,' said Cameron.

13

'Welcome to the Seelie court,' said a tall male fae with white hair and emerald green eyes. 'The Queen awaits you.'

He stepped back and waved his arm in an expansive welcoming gesture that beckoned me forward. I resisted for a short time, because the gesture reminded me of the barker who had tried to lead us onto the fairground rides.

'It's all right,' said Cameron. 'Go forward.'

Ahead was a tall white wall with a shining silver door in the centre. The door opened, and I looked beyond it to see a large chamber, decked out with romantic, flowering trees that twisted and turned into seating. The trees created a throne that had a bed of daisies as its cushion.

'Mr Cameron, your debt to me is now repaid. You may leave. The demi-fae will show you your exit. I assume you will not want to return to Mr Black's island?'

'I'm happy to stay and leave when Miss Lightfoot does,' said Cameron.

'You are not invited to remain,' said the fae.

'Airell … why do you keep me waiting?' said a female voice. I looked back at the chamber and now saw Aleora sitting on the throne. She was stunning, and not at all the fragile captive I'd seen in the bowels of Haven Lee[3]. No, this was how Aleora had appeared to me at first, even though I had not known that she was merely a facsimile of herself controlled by the Old Ones.

'This way,' said Airell.

Her call allowed Cameron's imminent departure to be delayed. Even though I still did not trust him, I was glad he had remained.

We moved toward the open entrance of the chamber, and as we passed inside I experienced a peculiar sensation. It was as though we had entered a vacuum. The door closed behind us. Airell stood guard at its entrance. I wasn't sure if this was to stop us from leaving or to prevent anyone else from entering. It didn't matter either way. I was curious about why I was there.

Cameron bowed, and I noticed his glamour was gone. He was now very much a Kitsune, adopting also the mannerism of a traditional Japanese man instead of an English one. He glanced at me and blinked. I realised I too had changed, and wondered what it was he saw instead of my usual appearance.

I glanced down at my hands and saw that my fingernails had elongated. I could feel the full length of the feline fangs sitting comfortably over my bottom lip. I touched my face, half expecting to find cat fur, but felt just my skin.

Aleora waved her hand to the left, and there appeared a full length mirror.

I had to see myself, exposed as I was, for it could only help me to understand my true nature.

I did not need to move, though, for just the mere wish

---

[3] See *Kat of Green Tentacles*.

of looking into it brought the mirror before me.

'Intriguing. More cat than vampire,' said Aleora, 'though there is still the taint of those creatures in you.'

She was right: the vampire venom was still in my veins, and in this unnatural light I could see it pulsing at my throat and on my wrists. I looked human, though, other than for the fangs and long nails. But standing as I was in my male britches, I could not be compared to other women of my age. No, I appeared to be older – around my eyes especially. There was the age of knowledge in them, for I had seen so much in my short lifetime. There was evidence too of some inner strength of the kind that one might see in the demeanour of an Olympian warrior.

'Yes,' Aleora said. 'You see it, don't you?'

'What does it mean?' I asked.

'You are not mortal anymore, Miss Lightfoot. In fact, I doubt you've aged a day since the cat gave you the power of Bastet. It saved you. It also made you something else.'

'*Bastet*?'

'A cat queen with great power. An old and powerful soul.'

'I'm *immortal*?' I said.

'Not quite, but close. Very close.'

Aleora waved her arm again, and the mirror vanished. In its place were two seats that looked as though they had been grown from tree roots.

'For your comfort,' Aleora said.

I was still taking in the Seelie queen's revelation of my nature, and so, almost trancelike, I moved to the seat on the right, as Cameron took the one on the left.

'You wished to speak with me?' I said.

'You are fighting an eternal darkness,' said Aleora. 'The human realm does not often concern us. But when such evil begins to affect our own kind, then we must take action.'

'For some time, the demon realm has been finding a way into the human one. I don't see how this can affect your world, though,' I said.

'Neither did we. At first. And so we have, as is our nature, left you to fight your own battles. Now, however, it had become necessary for us to engage with it.'

'Why?' I asked. 'What's happened?'

Airell spoke up then. 'My Queen has been attacked.'

'By whom?' asked Cameron.

'Not whom. *What,*' said Airell.

He moved away from the door and came to stand beside Aleora. A second throne appeared, and he took his place beside her. It was then I understood what he was to Aleora. He was her consort, and he would do whatever he had to do to protect her.

'Airell speaks of the evil you have been fighting all along. And evil that comes not from a demon realm, but from the emptiness of man.'

'What do you mean?' I asked.

'When men lost their souls, the darkness filled the space. It became sentient. It is a parasite that spreads. It eats away at the spirit of those who are not empty, until they become as it is. A hollow. A void. A nothing. A black hole of darkness that cannot be made light.'

'In human religious belief we would call the darkness the devil,' I said.

'It does not matter what you call it. It is real because man has made it so.'

'How then does this harm your realm?' I asked again. As Cameron had said, the fae rarely spoke in straight terms. There was always a mystery. But I was determined to repeat the question enough that Aleora had to answer. 'How were *you* attacked?'

'Some of my people have been … overwhelmed … by the darkness. It appears to them as a human female or male of great beauty. You know we are attracted to splendour. We like to take and keep such divine humans at times. But these creatures … take us … First in fascination, which becomes obsession. Then in melancholy. Those infected wither and pine for the beauty they saw but could not have. I am connected to all of my kind. This is how I am attacked. Through my people. The Sidhe have no soul. We live forever and have no need of one. But this darkness gets inside the essence that gives us life. It eats away at it. It changes who we are. And once changed, these beings infect others. I can taste the taint flowing through the blood of my people – it is a bitter poison on my tongue.'

I took this in for a moment. Thinking through the dilemma of the darkness possessing the immortal form of the Sidhe. It was not a good scenario.

'How do we fight it?' I asked.

'*You* must *infect* the source, Miss Lightfoot. You must destroy it with your blood,' said Aleora.

'*Me*? I can only destroy these creatures one at a time.'

'The cats gave you the gift of Bastet,' said Airell. 'The darkness came before, and Bastet beat it back with her army of felines. They have been, and will remain, your allies. The darkness has returned, and now you are the one that has to save us all.'

'How do you know all this?'

'Bastet was once ours,' said Aleora. 'She occupied the human realm at the birth of the Egyptian empire. She warned me. She said it would return.'

'If you can talk to Bastet, then surely you can get her to help again,' I reasoned.

Aleora smiled. 'My dear girl, I *am* talking to her. Right

now. Don't you realise? You are her. You've always been her. Reborn over and over again to await this moment in time.'

I experienced a moment of displacement again, and the world shifted and turned. It was, I thought, the shock of Aleora's revelation.

'I can't be,' I said.

Cameron took my hand.

We were no longer in the throne room. Aleora and Airell were gone. We were standing by a tree in the middle of the expansive underworld forest.

'What's going on?' I said.

'You have to kill the darkness,' said Cameron.

'But how? If we kill Staton he'll just move into another body.'

'You're confused. But it will all come back to you soon,' explained Cameron. His eyes were kind.

Edward Brewster and his wife, Cerys, were standing by the tree as though they had been waiting for us. I frowned. This was all so confusing.

'What are you doing here?' I said, and then I remembered.

Edward Brewster. Of course!

Brewster had appeared in many guises throughout my adventures. First as a security guard at Tiffany's, next as the man who had sacrificed himself to save the life of a slave on the Pollitt plantation. Another time he had appeared as a bellhop at Chateau Chantal, where Pepper and I had almost married. When I was helping to find the missing girls of Haven Lee, Brewster had been my fae rescuer – he had found me trapped in the cellar. Finally, in our adventure in Spain, Brewster had appeared as a doctor. In all cases he had always proved to be trustworthy and had died for his efforts.

It was extraordinary, however, that after each and every contact, I had completely forgotten about him. Of course he had changed his appearance in each reincarnation, deliberately avoiding jogging my memory of him before. But he had always used the same name. How could I have failed to realise?

'I think you have some explaining to do,' I said. 'You're no army deserter. You've just been telling me everything you thought I wanted to hear.'

'I'm only ever here to serve …' he said, bowing. 'Now, I need to return you to the island.'

My heart sank. Pepper and Martin! Oh God! They *must* have been injured, at the very least, by the explosion on Carey's boat.

'Remember,' said Cameron, reading me with those sharp fox eyes of his, 'it's not *where* we go but *when?*'

14

'When I open the door we'll have only a few minutes,' Brewster said. 'Mr Pepper and Mr Crewe will already be making their way to the jetty. If you hurry, you can stop them before the explosion.'

'But what about the others?' I asked.

'Others?'

'Yes. The demons that have already died. If we can pass through a doorway that leads me back to the moment that Martin and Pepper are ... well, can we go back any sooner?'

Brewster was silent a moment. Then he said, 'Yes. We can. But I thought ...'

'You think perhaps they deserved to die?' I asked.

'Not all of them,' Brewster shrugged.

'It's all or nothing.'

Brewster nodded. 'Okay. Let's do it. We need to catch Staton before he kills Tessier ... Maybe we can end it there. But there's something else you need to know, Miss Lightfoot.'

'What's that?'

'We can't meet up with ourselves. We'll need to be very careful.'

Brewster kissed his wife, then he turned around in the forest three times.

'What is he doing?' I asked.

'He's locating the right door for the right place and time,' Cerys said. 'It's an art that few of us can practise, but is one of Edward's particular skills.'

'There …' said Brewster, after the third turn.

He walked away from Cerys and deeper into the forest. It was midnight again, and the moon shone down between the trees, illuminating a pathway. Brewster traversed the path as though he were approaching a holy shrine. I followed him. He stopped walking and stared ahead. Then he raised a hand and waved it before him.

A dull ember of light, the size of a firefly, appeared ahead of us. Then it began to expand outwards until its shine fell directly upon us. There was a whoosh of sound, as if a million bees were buzzing around our heads.

'What about Mr Cameron?' I said.

'He has his own path to choose …'

The light grew so bright that I was forced to close my eyes; and then, with a brilliant flash, we were no longer in the underground.

I stepped out of the light into natural daylight. 'Where are we?'

'Look!'

I opened my eyes. We were stood at the top of the hill on Carnasie Pol. Below us were the jetty and the stretch of water between the island and the mainland. I could see a boat approaching.

'Hide,' said Brewster. 'We are a little earlier than I planned. But perhaps that is just as well.'

'It's our arrival on the island,' I said.

'Yes.'

We ducked down behind the sharp rocks and watched as the boat docked and everyone disembarked. I saw myself jumping from the gangplank and watched as Martin and I followed the others up to the house.

'Pepper's already here,' I said. 'I suppose I could have found him … warned him what was going to happen.'

'There's no time,' said Brewster.

'Where is Tessier?'

'He arrived earlier also,' said Brewster.

The party went inside the house, and Brewster and I traversed the rock path downwards. We looked into the window by the door and saw the group gathered. They were captivated by Grace Monroe, and now I saw her spider nature clearly.

The party dispersed, and I tried not to think about what we had done during that time. I focused instead on what we had to do now. We needed to find Tessier, and warn him not to drink the brandy that night.

Down on the jetty I now saw Tessier standing watching the boat as it made its way back across the water to the mainland.

'There he is,' I said. 'I need to talk to him now.'

'Wait,' said Brewster. 'I came out to him. We can't meet ourselves, remember.'

I saw Brewster's earlier self walking now toward Tessier. They talked for a moment, then Brewster walked away.

'What did you say to him?'

'Only that dinner would be served in an hour's time.'

'Maybe this is my moment …'

I hurried down the steps two at a time and reached the jetty as Tessier was making his way back. Then Tessier turned and looked at me.

'You *can't* be here right now,' Tessier said.

I took a step back, shocked at Tessier's rage-filled expression. Then I understood what it was … His eyes glowed. He was the darkness. Tessier was the darkness, not Staton.

'I'm sorry. I was looking for Mr Brewster. I wanted some water …' I mumbled, pretending to be my earlier self.

'That way,' Tessier said, waving his arm toward the house. But his eyes were fierce with the flame of the darkness.

I backed away and turned back to the house.

Back up the steps I found Brewster where I'd left him.

'Tessier is the darkness. Not Staton.'

'But … you saw the darkness in Staton.'

'I know. It doesn't make sense.'

We watched from our vantage point as Tessier went back inside the house.

'If the darkness is in Tessier, he's a lost cause,' said Brewster.

'Not necessarily. We have to catch Tessier at the moment when the darkness leaves him. Then warn him about the poison.'

'Or,' said Brewster, 'you put the poison into Tessier's glass *before* …'

I knew then that Tessier probably couldn't be saved, but possibly Staton could. After all, before the darkness entered him, he was probably just an ordinary man. We knew that the darkness would twist the facts regarding the demons inside. So why couldn't Staton be totally innocent of any crime? Besides, without the darkness operating him, he wasn't even technically a demon!

I had a plan, and I told it to Brewster. Then I checked my pocket watch.

'We have half an hour before everyone gathers for dinner. Then you were serving drinks and cigars to the men, weren't you?' I said to Brewster.

'Yes. I was going to. But then you came into the kitchen and asked me for some port for the ladies …'

'I didn't,' I said.

'Oh.'

I frowned. 'Obviously I'm going to.'

We waited and watched from the windows outside as the party gathered and then went into the dining-room. When everyone was out of the way, I went upstairs into the room I had been allocated and pulled out another dress from my trunk. It was similar to the one I was wearing downstairs at that moment. As all of my formal wear had been adapted to drape conveniently over my breeches, and because I wasn't really concerned about fashion, I tended to chose similar fabrics and colours.

I met Brewster back outside, just before the ladies came out of the dining room and headed to the parlour.

While the men were lighting their cigars, I followed the old Brewster into the kitchen and asked him for port for the ladies.

'Of course, Miss,' he said, and he hurried away with a tray and glasses. Then, the future Brewster came into the kitchen. He picked up the tray that his previous self had been preparing.

'Here,' I said.

'What is it?' Brewster asked, looking suspiciously at the phial of white powder I held out to him.

'Arsenic powder. I make a solution out of it to soak my hands in when I'm having trouble removing the stain of gunpowder,' I explained. 'Put a little in Tessier's glass. We need to kill him before the darkness finds another victim.'

'Are you sure that will work?'

I wasn't, but I nodded. Then I poured a little brandy into all of the glasses, while Brewster held the tray.

Brewster went away to serve the drinks, making sure that Tessier was last. I waited outside the dining-room door and listened to the men talk.

'Let's join the ladies, shall we?' I heard Pepper say. 'We can take the drinks with us.'

The others agreed, and Tessier walked out, followed by Staton, Pepper, Martin, Walsh, Khan and Clark, with his untouched drink.

Brewster and I slipped back into the kitchen before they passed.

'There's a secret passage,' said Brewster. 'I'm not supposed to know of it, but the missus and I went exploring when we first arrived. This way.'

In the hallway, Brewster moved a candelabra, and a panel in the wall slid silently open. I had been in many places where secret passages were part of the structure of a house, so I was unsurprised to find one in this purpose-built residence. It did occur to me to wonder, however, how long the darkness had been planning this whole venture. Surely it had started when he began to wear the body of Black?

Brewster opened a panel, and suddenly we were staring into the parlour.

'There's a mirror on the other side,' Brewster explained.

In the parlour, Tessier promptly died to plan.

'It's over, then!' I said.

'It might be. But we had better make sure. Time to take another leap. This time a little forward.'

15

Brewster closed the panel to the parlour and began to turn on the spot. Bright light broke into the hidden passageway. I saw the moonlit pathway light up again. Then the underworld forest appeared ahead of us.

'Stay close beside me,' Brewster said.

We barely took two steps, and then the light disappeared and I found we were once more in the passageway in the walls of the house at Carnarsie Pol.

Brewster opened the panel again, and we now saw an empty parlour. Daylight streamed through the windows.

'It's morning. And if I'm not mistaken, everyone is now gathering in the dining-room for breakfast. This way, Miss Lightfoot.'

I followed Brewster down the passageway until he stopped beside another panel.

'If we really have killed the darkness, then Staton should still be sleeping soundly in his bed,' I said.

'Yes, and Katie Meyers will have no reason to try to escape through the mirror.'

We opened this panel and saw our past selves, preparing to eat breakfast with the remaining demons. Then a scream echoed through the house.

We remained watching as everyone rushed from the room. We knew it was too late for Staton. That meant of course that he was now on course to being fully possessed by the darkness.

'I'm not sure what this means,' said Brewster.

'Staton is perhaps already the darkness. He could have faked his own death.'

'No,' said Brewster. 'I saw those wounds. No human, even a possessed one, could survive injuries like that.'

'Then someone else killed him ...' I said.

I hissed, taking a step back. Katie Meyers was staring into the mirror above the fireplace as though she could see us on the other side.

'She's already contemplating her escape,' Brewster said.

'Look at her eyes.'

'Oh no!' said Brewster. 'The darkness has already moved.'

Katie Meyers was holding the essence of evil now, firmly inside her. It was very likely that she had killed Staton.

'What do we do?' I wondered.

'That explains why Meyers was so keen to leave ...' Brewster said.

'I don't understand,' I said.

'The darkness knows we are here. That we are trying to destroy it.'

'But this is *his* game ... He's calling all the shots, and everyone here is trapped.'

'True,' said Brewster. 'But while he's in human form, so is he.'

But the darkness was no longer inside a human, he was now possessing a fae, and the Sidhe can always find their way home. Knowing it had been foiled, the evil inside her would use Katie's knowledge and escape, leaving us to our own devices. But we couldn't let him leave, even if it meant destroying Katie's body.

The scene we had already lived through replayed before us, and then came the moment when Katie Meyers announced to the room that she was leaving.

From behind the mirror we saw the portal open.

'No!' I cried, pressing my hand against the panel.

As Katie began to pass through, there was a moment when I knew she saw us on the other side. Then her face contorted.

'You!' she gasped into the collapsing void.

My fingers grew hot, I felt a burst of energy exploding form the palm of my hand, and then I saw the mirror gateway falter. The glass froze and Katie's head fell into the passageway, dropping and rolling to come to a halt by Brewster's feet.

'What happened?' I said.

'You did,' answered Brewster. 'You blocked her from leaving. Maybe now the darkness is thwarted. But there's only one way to find out. We need to move forward again.'

I closed my eyes as Brewster began to turn on the spot. I was overwhelmed with guilt at the death of Katie Meyers. Even though we knew we couldn't let the darkness escape, I hadn't intended to be the cause of her demise.

'Where now?' I asked.

'We need to see what occurred between Grace Monroe and Khan.'

'You think maybe one of them is the darkness?'

Brewster didn't answer; he was concentrating hard on our destination. I noticed that this time he did a quarter less turn than the usual full three times.

The light, pathway and forest came, only this time they were less clear than before.

'I've allowed us a little more time. We have to get out of the house and down to the water's edge before Monroe tries to bespell Khan.'

We emerged this time outside. I began to run down the rocky steps toward the jetty. Then we saw Walsh. He was in the water. Under normal circumstances I doubt I'd have been able to see a night shade – especially during the daytime. There were no shadows in the water to hide in, but the water clung to his skin like liquid gold. Fortunately, Walsh didn't know he was being observed. It was then I knew that Walsh no longer in the driving seat of his own body, ethereal or corporeal. The darkness showed through every drop of water as a blue-black flame. Its evil was irrepressible.

Walsh hadn't seen us. I reached the side of the house, and there I saw the axe, abandoned by the woodpile. I picked it up.

'Do you see him?' I asked Brewster.

'Yes.'

'We need surprise on our side. Can you get me closer without him seeing me?'

Brewster nodded and then paused. A second later he had made a small movement. Not quite a turn, but a fraction of one. I rushed down the light-flooded pathway and emerged swinging the axe. Walsh was in the process of solidifying as I swung. He wasn't fully formed, or perhaps the axe wouldn't have done such a good job. The blade landed in his spine, and I had my superhuman cat-vampire strength behind it, as well as the propulsion from the time portal.

The axe went clean through him. Cutting Walsh in

half. As the two parts of his body fell back from the pier into the water, his body fully formed. The night shade in him was as dead as the man he had once been.

'Come on,' said Brewster by my side. 'We haven't long. Monroe and Khan should be down this way.'

At that moment Brewster and I heard voices. We ducked away from the pier and hid behind the sharp rocks that obviously acted as breakers when the tide came in.

'It's Grace and Khan,' I said. 'We were earlier than we thought.'

'Miss Monroe,' Khan was saying, 'I find it difficult to believe that you haven't met Mr Black. I mean, how can you work for someone that you don't know?'

'Black pays me well. He also offered me a job at a time when it was convenient for me to esc … *leave* England.'

They walked on in silence, and then Grace stopped. She doubled over as though in terrible pain.

'Miss Monroe, are you all right?' Khan said.

Grace stood upright, and then Khan found himself in her thrall; but he wasn't the only one. As Brewster watched her, he too became incapable of moving, and I also struggled to form cohesive thought.

I shook my head, trying to shift the fugue that suddenly hovered around it. Grace's influence was stronger even than it had been the day before, and I began to focus on why.

My mind cleared enough to understand that this was not a normal reaction to her. It was as though her hypnosis was exaggerated. She was a flame to Khan's moth, and we too might be caught in its heat.

'Ouch!'

I looked down at my hand. A bee fell to the floor by my feet and promptly died.

I pulled the sting out of the back of my hand, and then noticed the beehive a few feet away from where Brewster and I had hidden.

An unreasonable rage over came me. It shook away the last of Grace's spell. I turned to the beehive, holding up my stung hand as though to point out to its occupants the error their co-worker had made.

The swarm surged out of the hive and hovered before my hand.

I heard a cry behind me. Glancing over my shoulder, I saw Grace, her arms now around Khan, as she attempted to press her vile fanged mouth against his.

I turned suddenly. The hand that had appeared to hold back the bees now pointed to the couple. The bees flew up and over my head and straight for Grace.

They fell upon her, without mercy, as though she had been the culprit who had disturbed their hive. Khan, true to his explanation of events, did indeed try to save the woman, and was stung several times. Then he began to call for help. Grace's body twitched as she fell to the ground. But the bees didn't let up. The few that had not previously reached her now dived and stung in one final attack.

I saw Grace turning into her spider form. Her single arms split and divided into four on each side. I also saw something else. The essence of a dark presence lifted from her – like Walsh's shade – and disappeared before I could give chase.

16

Brewster took a while to come out of the black widow's induced trance.

'As I killed Walsh, the darkness fled him,' I said. 'I'm just not quick enough to stop him.'

'Don't be so hard on yourself,' Brewster said. 'We weren't to know that the darkness had possessed all of these demons in turn.'

'But we do know where he ended up,' I said. 'How do you feel?'

'Confused. It was like Grace's power, but so much stronger …'

'It seems that the darkness uses everyone's strengths once it's inside them.'

I sat down on the rocks beside Brewster. I was drained. I couldn't understand why the bees had attacked Grace, or why one had randomly stung me. But if it hadn't been for that sting, I might have been unable to fight the black widow's influence.

'You controlled the bees …' Brewster said. 'That much is clear. And you sent them to stop her.'

'But I didn't know she was the darkness.'

'Something inside you did,' Brewster said.

I tried thinking back to Aleora's words. She had told me something important. I could remember bits of it. I was reincarnated. Bastet. The cats had changed me; or had they just brought Bastet out … to become part of me?

It was all still so vague. And Cameron had said something else, before he had disappeared for his own mission. He'd said it would all come back when the time was right. That I'd know what to do.

'Miss Lightfoot,' said Brewster, 'I think we ought to try just to save your friends. There seems no point in looking to save those whose deaths we *know* have happened.'

'What do you mean? There is still always a chance …'

'Miss, we can't change the past. We know that Mr Matthewman and Miss Shafer die … But neither of us actually saw the boat explode.'

I knew that Brewster was right, but I couldn't leave without seeing what had happened in the moments before Matthewman's change into a werewolf, and Shafer's medusa transformation.

'Please, Mr Brewster,' I said.

Brewster brought us out seconds before the change began to take Matthewman. I heard again his cried warning and saw our past selves running toward the house. Jessica Shafer however appeared unafraid, and she remained behind. It was then I saw the burning embers of darkness in Matthewman's eyes, and I knew without doubt that this poor man had been taken by the creature when it left Grace's dying body.

Out of everyone, I felt the most sympathy for Matthewman. Here was a man who had been cursed through no apparent fault of his own. He had lost the woman he loved, and lived with the awful guilt of her death on his conscience.

I made to hurry to them, but Brewster held me back.

'You need to chose you battles carefully now, Miss. You can't win against Shafer. But she will take the darkness down in this form.'

And so we let the scene play out as it had before, with no interference from us.

'I'll take you to hell with me,' Shafer said as Matthewman crushed her in his powerful wolf arms.

And she did.

I took Brewster's hand as the survivors came out and began to build their funeral pyre. I hadn't realised how fitting a tribute this had been to all of those fallen in the path of the darkness.

'It's time,' I said as I watched the last embers blowing out to sea.

Brewster began to turn around. Then we were right back where the fae queen had wanted us to go all along.

I rushed down the steps, shouting and waving my hands. Pepper stopped and turned to see me running toward him.

'Get away from the jetty!' I said.

Pepper didn't hesitate. He hurried back up the steps, quickly followed by Martin, Khan and Harvey. They were halfway back when Carey's boat reached the jetty.

I could see Carey raise his arm. He wore a vest laced with sticks of dynamite, and now he lit the fuse that was attached to them all.

'No, Captain Carey!' I yelled. 'You don't have to die for the darkness.'

But Carey's eyes were already empty, and I knew he'd been consumed by the parasitical evil. The explosion rocked the mountainside, but fortunately the men were far enough away that they escaped injury.

Pepper and Martin took the steps two at a time and were soon at my side.

'No time to explain, follow me!' I said.

I turned and ran back up to the mansion with Pepper and Martin at my heels. Once inside the house I led them toward the kitchen and into the servants' quarters.

A blast of light reflected into the corridor from Brewster's room, followed by the sound of gunshots and breaking glass. I stopped in the corridor and indicated for the men to wait until the light went out. Then we carried on into the room.

Staton was where I had left him. He turned in surprise, and then that slow evil smile was back on his face.

'Miss Lightfoot, you have proved to be far more resourceful than I expected. You've hounded me from every soul I tried to take, forcing me into this already rotting carcase.'

He raised the gun and pointed it at me.

'You can't kill me,' I said.

He fired. I felt no pain, but I looked at my stomach, half expecting to see a hole there.

'Kat!'

I turned to see Pepper slumping. Blood blossomed on his chest. Martin bent to him.

'There are more ways than one to skin a cat ...' the darkness said.

My fangs burst from my gums and I dived at Staton. We tussled. The gun went off again, but neither of us was hit. As we fought, the weapon fell from Staton's hands.

He was stronger than he looked, but then he did have the darkness inside him. I knocked him to the floor and rolled, my hands around his throat as I tried to choke the evil life-force from him.

The insidious light flickered behind Staton's eyes. I saw the darkness, fully housed within the man, and I knew this might be my only opportunity to end this supernatural evil on earth. He heaved his body, throwing me off as easily as if I were an insect bothering him on a hot summer night.

'There is nothing in this lifetime that can destroy me, Miss Lightfoot,' he said.

But I knew better. I remembered. Finally. Not just what Aleora and Airell had said, but something else. I had the knowledge of Bastet buried inside my soul, and now she told me what to do.

I got back to my feet, and then I bit into my own arm, shredding the vein at my wrist. With a sweep of my arm I flicked my tainted blood over Staton.

It was as though liquid fire had touched him. The darkness screamed through the mouth of Staton. And then the red blood ignited and the flames licked up his face and caught in his hair.

He fought it. Dropping to the floor, he rolled, trying to put out the fire that consumed him. But it was to no avail. Then I saw the evil glimmer inside Staton's eyes as it squirmed and writhed. It tried to escape this host body, as it had left all the others before, but it couldn't. You see, as soon as my blood had touched Staton's body it had also reached inside to take hold of the darkness within him. The darkness could not escape. Trapping the evil within a dying body was the only way to destroy it.

The fire did not touch any part of the room, but it swallowed Staton. But even while he burned, he tried to reach out to take me with him. He crawled on hands and knees as I backed out of reach, but the physical strength of the human frame he was carrying gave out before he could reach me. I moved lightly on the balls of my feet as the creature thrashed and raved, keeping just out of reach until the body could move no more.

Then I stood and watched it dissolve in on itself. A carcass of ichor, black burnt blood, and the stench of sulphur wafted into the air from the remains.

I helped Martin pull the stricken Pepper into the corridor, and from there we watched as my blood completely disintegrated the evil that had been plaguing us for years.

Pepper groaned, and I came back to the reality of his injury. Was it serious?

I knelt beside him and examined the wound. I knew immediately it was bad.

'The darkness is no more,' said Harvey from the end of the corridor. 'I can feel it … gone.'

I nodded. 'Ursula and Almia can be yours now.'

'My ship is on its way,' Khan told him. 'Let me take you to her.'

The merman shook Khan's hand in gratitude.

'And we shall be friends under the sea as well as above it. Such wonders I may show you, Captain Nemo,' Harvey said.

Even as this new friendship was forged, I wondered if my old friend would die. Pepper didn't look good. I had no idea how to help him.

'Martin?' I said, for the first time feeling helpless. 'I can't lose him.'

Khan's ship arrived, and he invited us on board. Two of his crewmen carried Pepper inside on a gurney with great care. The darkness might have been gone, but my life was still in turmoil. Pepper slipped in and out of consciousness, and as we descended into the bowels of the magnificent *Nautilus* I had no desire to look at anything but him.

'You're wounded,' said Nemo. (It seemed appropriate to use his seafaring name once we had boarded the ship.) 'My physician will help you both.'

'No. I'm fine. I'm healed already,' I pointed out.

'You are a miracle, Miss Lightfoot.'

Nemo's physician looked grim as he examined Pepper's wound. There was a bullet lodged in his heart. The prognosis was not good.

I stayed beside him in the *Nautilus*'s medical room, afraid to let go of his hand lest he slip away from me.

'Don't leave me, George,' I said.

Martin retreated from the room, and so did Nemo and Harvey, as though they were leaving me to my grief. But Pepper wasn't dead, and I wasn't ready yet to let him go.

I ran the events of the past few days and hours through my head, as though by replaying these thoughts I might find some miraculous solution.

Aleora had said I was very close to immortal. My blood was powerful and could destroy evil. What if it could also grant life? What if I could share my invulnerability with Pepper? Just as the cats had passed it onto me? With the memories endowed by Bastet, I knew this was at least possible.

Pepper had been bitten by a vampire too, hadn't he?

I put my head against his and whispered my thoughts like a prayer or a promise.

'I give you what I have …' And then I bit into my wrist and placed my potent blood against Pepper's lips.

Pepper didn't move. For a time his stillness scared me. Had I waited too long?

'Drink, George,' I said. Then I prised open his mouth and dropped spots of my blood inside.

Nothing happened, so I slashed my wrist again, deeper this time, so the blood would flow faster.

I pressed it against his mouth and filled it with my blood. Pepper didn't move. He neither choked nor swallowed.

I had to accept that it was too late. Pepper was gone to me, and there was no bringing him back.

I put my head down on him and cried.

17

'We'll bury him at sea,' said Nemo. 'It's the least we can do for such an admirable man.'

My eyes had been dry when I had told them Pepper was gone. I had refused the comfort of Martin, who had now left me with Harvey and Nemo while he had gone to say his goodbyes to Pepper's body. The *Nautilus* was preparing to dive once more, now that it was in open sea.

'What about Mr Cameron?' asked Harvey, after I explained to them what had happened.

'He left the underground by another door. I suspect he is now in Russia,' I said.

Nemo and Harvey looked at me. They didn't ask why the Kitsune, Paul Cameron, would want to go to Russia. But I knew he'd be looking for revenge. Cameron was an honourable man, just as all of the remaining demons were.

Pepper's watery funeral was planned *en route* to Cornwall, where Harvey hoped to be reunited with Ursula and her cousin Almia. I hoped they would still be waiting for him, for I wished that someone in this adventure could enjoy a happy ending.

Like Harvey, I could feel the absence of the darkness,

but at a time when we could otherwise have celebrated, I was left in the position of not caring for the future after all. Without Pepper, I didn't think it mattered.

If the darkness was gone, Martin and I could finally retire, have a normal life. I could feel confident that my young sister Sally would grow up in a world of normal human evil, which we could anticipate and protect ourselves against, and not the unpredictable supernatural kind. The irony that Pepper and I could have finally led a normal life together too was not lost on me. And I was consumed with regret, which weighed me down further than my already severe sadness.

I let Nemo's and Harvey's conversation fade away and dropped into my mind. I saw a world without demons, where Mr Pepper, my next door neighbour, would have eventually invited me to walk with him. In that world, I would have shyly said 'Yes,' and Mother and Sally would have sat with us as chaperones until such a time as Pepper proposed and we walked, without supernatural interference, down the aisle together.

I squeezed my eyes shut, pushing back the tears. I was not given to sentimentality. Not after all I'd seen. And crying, I had always thought, showed weakness. But now I no longer believed that. Instead I felt that tears would be an acceptance that this was the end. I didn't want to give in to that final certainty, so I swallowed and held them back.

Someone took my hand as I sat in the corner of Nemo's sitting-room. I thought it must be Martin, refusing to accept my rejection of his comfort. But a shiver ran through my fingers, up my arm – a feeling of profound *recognition*. This person was *like* me.

I kept my eyes closed for a moment longer, daring to hold on to this fervent wish.

'Kat?'

I sighed. How could I now hear his voice? Was this a dream? Had I collapsed in exhaustion after all? Had I lost my mind with grief?

'Kat?'

I opened my eyes, and they blurred with the unshed tears.

'You saved me,' he said.

'*Pepper*?'

'Yes.'

Nemo performed the wedding ceremony. Mother and Sally could plan us a big party when we returned to New York, if it made them happy. For now it was our time, and I couldn't wait to start my new life as George Pepper's wife.

For a honeymoon we travelled on the *Nautilus* to England to see Harvey Clark reunited with his love.

The day we arrived, Pepper and I were full of excitement, and also tense for Harvey.

'Miss Lightfoot,' said Nemo, passing me some curious waxy-looking substance. 'Press this into your ears. Just in case.'

But there was no need to worry, because I belonged to my soulmate now, and Harvey's song could never reach me.

But when he sent out the call on the coast of Cornwall I heard the music of angels, not dissimilar to the trumpets I'd heard in the Seelie court. And so it made me realise that all supernatural creatures, be they fae or mer, or indeed cat hybrids, were of similar ilk.

But the music drew someone special to Harvey. Someone who had waited and hoped he would return for the last seven years.

Harvey entered the water, and we watched through binoculars as Ursula swam into his arms. His touch transformed this somewhat plain girl into a beautiful sea maiden. Behind her, her companion Almia joined them. She too changed at Harvey's touch. They sang then. A joyous music that gave me hope for Harvey that he was right: Ursula would be the one to last.

The three of them sank into the water, never to be seen again. Though I suspected Nemo would cross paths with them at some point.

'Things will have changed,' said Martin. 'And my inventions will be no longer needed.'

'But Martin, you could still be an innovator. Just think what you could now bring to the world, in communication devices as well as weaponry,' said Pepper.

Martin smiled at me and then at my new husband.

'We all know it is different now. I have no desire to remain a "gooseberry in your apple pie".'

'Martin, you know that was just Black trying to divide us,' I said.

'I've been speaking with Nemo. He could use someone like me on board. When I'm on land again, I'll look you up,' he replied.

We couldn't change his mind, and so we said goodbye to him at New York docks. Nemo had brought us home so that I could see my mother and sister and tell them the news that they had always wanted to hear.

As for George and me?

I am no longer 'very close' to immortality. We share half each of my former invulnerability. I don't know exactly what this means for the future, but I suspect we shall both live very long lives, and age slower than most. If injured we heal quickly and without scar, but not instantly as I once did. But I had made a pact when I gave him half of what the cats gave me. I knew that living forever without Pepper would be a curse and not a gift. I wasn't strong enough to bear it.

And so, we live as half-immortals. Strong together and free at last from the darkness that once tried to consume us.

About the Author

Award winning author Sam Stone began her professional writing career in 2007 when her first novel won the Silver Award for Best Novel with *ForeWord Magazine* Book of the Year Awards. Since then she has gone on to write several novels, three novellas and many short stories. She was the first woman in 31 years to win the British Fantasy Society Award for Best Novel. She also won the award for Best Short Fiction in the same year (2011).

Stone loves all types of fiction and enjoys mixing horror (her first passion) with a variety of different genres including science fiction, fantasy and Steampunk.

Her works can be found in paperback, audio, screen and eBook.

More Telos Titles
By Sam Stone

<u>KAT LIGHTFOOT SERIES</u>
Steampunk, horror, adventure series
1: ZOMBIES AT TIFFANY'S
2: KAT ON A HOT TIN AIRSHIP
3: WHAT'S DEAD PUSSYKAT
4: KAT OF GREEN TENTACLES
5: KAT AND THE PENDULUM
6: TEN LITTLE DEMONS
THE COMPLETE KAT LIGHTFOOT

<u>JINX CHRONICLES</u>
Hi-tech science fiction fantasy trilogy
1: JINX TOWN
2: JINX MAGIC
3: JINX BOUND

<u>THE VAMPIRE GENE SERIES</u>
Horror, fantasy time-travel thrillers
1: KILLING KISS
2: FUTILE FLAME
3: DEMON DANCE
4: HATEFUL HEART
5: SILENT SAND
6: JADED JEWEL

THE DARKNESS WITHIN: FINAL CUT
Science fiction horror short novel

ZOMBIES IN NEW YORK
AND OTHER BLOODY JOTTINGS
Thirteen stories of horror and passion and six
mythological and erotic poems from the pen of the new
Queen of Vampire fiction.

CTHULHU AND OTHER MONSTERS
20 Tales of Horror and Cosmic Terror

Telos Publishing
www.telos.co.uk

Other Titles By Sam Stone

POSING FOR PICASSO

Other Telos Steampunk and Horror Titles

TANITH LEE
BLOOD 20
20 Vampire Stories through the ages

TANITH LEE A-Z (forthcoming)
*An A-Z collection of Short Fiction by renowned writer
Tanith Lee*

GRAHAM MASTERTON
THE HELL CANDIDATE
THE DJINN
THE WELLS OF HELL
RULES OF DUEL (With William S Burroughs)

PAUL FINCH
CAPE WRATH AND THE HELLION (Horror Novella)
TERROR TALES OF CORNWALL (Ed. Paul Finch)
TERROR TALES OF THE NORTH WEST OF ENGLAND
(Ed. Paul Finch) (Forthcoming)

DAVID J HOWE
TALESPINNING
Collection of stories, novel fragments and more

SIMON CLARK
HUMPTY'S BONES
THE FALL

<u>FREDA WARRINGTON</u>
NIGHTS OF BLOOD WINE
Vampire Horror Short Story Collection

<u>RAVEN DANE</u>
THE MISADVENTURES OF CYRUS DARIAN
Steampunk Adventure Series
1: CYRUS DARIAN AND THE TECHNOMICRON
2: CYRUS DARIAN AND THE GHASTLY HORDE
3: CYRUS DARIAN AND THE DEMON (Forthcoming)

DEATH'S DARK WINGS
Alternative History Novel

ABSINTHE AND ARSENIC
Horror and Fantasy Short Story Collection

<u>PAUL LEWIS</u>
SMALL GHOSTS
Horror Novella

<u>STEPHEN LAWS</u>
SPECTRE

<u>RHYS HUGHES</u>
CAPTAINS STUPENDOUS

<u>HELEN MCCABE</u>
THE PIPER TRILOGY
1: PIPER
2: THE PIERCING
3: THE CODEX

<u>SOLOMON STRANGE</u>
THE HAUNTING OF GOSPALL

<u>DAWN G HARRIS</u>
DIVINER

TELOS PUBLISHING
www.telos.co.uk